Praises for

Five Stars! Hot!

"OMG!!! Devi Sparks has written the HOTTEST, funniest, sexiest, most emotional book I've had the pleasure to read! Fairy Godlover has all the aspects of a true erotic romance; sex, laughter, sex, plot, sex, laughter, and love. Did I mention that this story was full of sex and laughter? ...One of the hottest stories I've read in a while... For a story that will wrap itself around not only your heart but your body, you will definitely want to pick up Devi Sparks' *Fairy Godlover*!"

—Vikky Bertling, *Just Erotic Romance Reviews*

Five Blue Ribbons!

"Devi Sparks debut novel, *Fairy Godlover* is outstanding! It is hard for me not to gush over how much I enjoyed reading this book.... These were some of the hottest love scenes I have read EVER!... I loved *Fairy Godlover*, and would recommend it to anyone who loves a heartwarming, character-driven story with explosive sex. This story is a fine example of what erotica is all about. Bravo, Ms. Sparks!"

—Miaka Chase, *Romance Junkies*

Five Stars! Orgasmic!

"Leather, high heels, mirrors and elevators--you'll see when you read the book. And, the carwash scene, Oh glory! Devi Sparks let it fly--the sparks I mean--in Fairy Godlover. An enticing read, I couldn't put it down. This hot love story made me sizzle... This book should come with the following warning label, 'Reading Will Cause Multiple Orgasms.'"

—Lorretta Hall, *Just Erotic Romance Reviews*

OTHER WORKS BY DEVI SPARKS
Published by Phaze

Animal Magnetism
Despearately Seeking Cupid

www.Phaze.com

Fairy Godlover

An erotic romance novel by

DEVI SPARKS

PHaZE

Cincinnati, Ohio

PHAZE

6470A Glenway Avenue, #109
Cincinnati, OH 45211-5222

This is a work of fiction. Names, places, characters and incidents are either the product of the author's imagination or are used fictitiously, and any resemblance to any actual persons, living or dead, organizations, events or locales is entirely coincidental.

Paperback ISBN 1-59426-510-0

Phaze is an imprint of Mundania Press, LLC.

Chapter One

Kelsey Schroder shoved into the front door of her house balancing mail, purse, travel mug and jacket in one arm as she struggled to remove the key from the lock with the other. With a jerk, the key came loose, but so did the jacket and travel mug. She groaned as the latter hit the floor and spilled cold coffee over the polished hardwood.

Muttering mild obscenities, she stepped over the mess and entered the kitchen, depositing everything else on the counter and grabbing the paper towel roll. Then she swiped the window cleaner from beneath the sink and walked back to the front hall.

She really needed to do something about that sticky lock, but what?

Just as she was finishing the cleanup, the phone rang. With a sigh, she stood, tossed the coffee-soaked towels into the trash, and reached for the cordless handset.

"Hello?"

"Hola chica! I was hoping you'd be home!"

"Hi Gina, I just walked in."

"How was your day?"

"Oh, you know. Same old story."

"Fulfilling, but boring as hell?"

"Yeah. How was yours?" Kelsey went to the refrigerator and got a bottle of water and a protein bar—her usual after-work snack.

"Fabulous! I got a promotion!"

"That's great! I didn't even know you were up for

"Neither did I. That's what makes it so cool!"

"So what's your new job?" she asked, still chewing.

"I'm the new Promotions Director! You know how I told you they said Amber was sick last week? She quit! Got a better offer from KSPT Denton."

"Well congratulations! Do you also get a raise?"

"You know it, girl! The down side is that I have to be at the station all weekend to do a crash course in the scope of Amber's job."

"Think long-term benefits and you'll breeze through it." Even as she said it, Kelsey smiled, knowing long-term thought wasn't exactly her friend's forte. She was a 'now' kind of person who lived each day to the fullest.

Kelsey had met Gina her freshman year of college, when Gina lived across the hall on the sixth floor of Mercy Hall. For subsequent years they had shared an apartment with an assortment of other girls.

Gina had always been the wild one, her personality much larger than her slight, five foot five frame. While Kelsey had earned her degree in accounting with a minor in mathematics, Gina had earned a degree in marketing with a minor in theater.

Now Gina had her dream job, and Kelsey had a fulfilling job.

"Um, Kels? Would you hate me too much if I bowed out of the banquet next week?"

"I suppose I can't be too upset as long as you don't ask for a refund on your plate." Kelsey kept her voice light, but she wanted her best friend to know she wasn't joking.

"Of course not. Gimme some credit, will ya?"

"Just making sure. So what is so much more important than a boring charity banquet? You get a hot date?"

"Yeah, I got a date, and he is definitely hot."

"I sure could use one of those."

"Yeah, well. Wishing doesn't get you anywhere, does it? You need to quit being a *closet* nympho and make time to go out there and find yourself a gorgeous virile man."

Kelsey grinned at the 'closet nympho' bit. Gina was probably the only other person on earth who knew about a certain blue box in her closet.

"Make time. Hmm... I've still not found a recipe for that."

"Eh, you're not such a great cook anyway."

"Don't I know it. And besides, I could have Mayor Kirkpatrick if I really wanted." She could almost hear Gina's eyes rolling in the brief silence.

"Yeah, well... if you want to get it on with *that*, we may have to seriously discuss your obscene level of desperation."

"And the fact that the only sex I get requires batteries is *not* obscene?" She slammed the bar wrapper into the trash can to punctuate her statement, even though Gina couldn't see it.

"We all hit dry spells, sweetie. Why do you think they make those things in the first place?"

"So tell me about your hottie."

"Oh, honey. I met him at the gym on Monday, and we went out to lunch yesterday. Ooh! He's the perfect gentleman, I tell you! He's going out of town this weekend, but he's taking me to lunch again on Monday..."

As Gina went on about how they were going to a Mavericks game on Thursday night—the night of the banquet, how his green eyes slayed her, how his dark spiky hair made him look dangerously sexy, kinda like the lead singer of Hoobastank, Kelsey picked up each piece of mail, inspected it briefly, and deposited it either into the recycling or back onto the counter in a separate pile.

"Is he a good kisser?"

"Pretty good, not the best I've had, not the worst—

Don't say it. He might be very capable in bed—and I intend to find out."

"What about his personality?"

"His what?" Gina joked.

"You know, that little thing inside that's pretty much who you are. Whether you're an arrogant bastard or not."

She picked up a sky-blue envelope printed with strange markings. It almost went into the recycle bin, but impulse made her examine it more closely.

"I can spot an arrogant bastard a mile away, thanks to your arduous relationship with Shithead."

"Ancient history, Gina. I was twenty-two then. I didn't know any better." Kelsey turned the envelope over in her hands. Faerie Guardians, Inc.? Who was Faerie Guardians, Inc., and why would she be getting a hand-addressed mailing? *Hand addressed?* She looked at the front again. *Hand addressed.*

Had she ordered something off the Internet? Was it another charity wanting donations? *Only one way to find out, Kels.*

She tore open the envelope, a little more apprehensive than she thought she should be, and pulled out a gleaming white piece of paper.

Dear Ms. Kelsey Schroder,

We are pleased to inform you that you have been chosen to benefit from the services of one of our award-winning guardians. Please expect arrival within twenty-four hours.

Sincerely, R.H. Mann

After reading the letter silently, Kelsey puzzled for a few moments, brows furrowed. Was this a practical joke? If she knew anyone who was prone to such diversions, she might think so.

In her ear, Gina was continuing to tell her about the nameless hottie's finer qualities.

"Hey Gina," Kelsey interrupted. "You know anything about…" she flipped the envelope over again to look at the return address, "Faerie Guardians, Inc.?"

"Fairy *what*?"

"Never mind. Probably just junk mail."

But she tossed the letter on top of the stack of mail, rather than in the recycling. Perhaps she'd have another look after she'd eaten something and done her nightly stress-relief workout.

"Oh, shit. My mother's on the other line. I gotta go."

"Tell her I said hello."

"Yeah, yeah. *If* I answer it."

"Bye Gina."

"Bye sweetie."

Kelsey put the cordless back in the handset to charge and smiled. Conversations with Gina always had a way of vitalizing her, perhaps because Gina seemed to ooze excess energy.

Closet nympho. *Hmph.* She grabbed a fresh bottle of water from the fridge and headed down the hall to her bedroom to change her clothes and do her daily workout. The envelope on the counter was forgotten, at least for the moment.

Forty-five minutes later, she pulled off her headphones and tossed her dead walkman into her wing-back chair, but didn't slow her pace on the treadmill. When the crap would they make batteries that lasted more than a few days?

To occupy her brain in the absence of music, she concentrated on the statistics flashing on the machine's display. Twenty-three minutes. One hundred twenty-nine calories. Two-point-six miles.

Combined with the resistance training she'd done with hand weights and an exercise ball, she would get a good workout tonight. Maybe she would reward herself with a small dish of ice cream.

She grinned at the thought, her mouth already watering.

Just then a glowing ball of light danced in the peripheral of her vision.

She blinked a few times to dissipate the light, then hit the 'slower' button a few times. Her vision sometimes did weird things when her blood pressure got too high or she had a sinus infection. Since her head felt fine, she stuck two fingers to her neck to check her pulse.

Fourteen, fifteen, sixteen… The ball of light abandoned the edge of her vision altogether and danced into the middle of her bedroom, plain as day.

Uhhh… Her jaw sagged to her chest as her feet stopped. The treadmill, however, kept going, carrying her backward until she stumbled off the back, yanking the safety cord attached to her wrist from its slot in the front of the machine.

Arms flailing, she regained her balance and looked again to the center of the room where the ball of light still danced.

Wow, I must have worked out harder than I thought. She closed her eyes and took a deep breath, counted to three, and opened them again.

Still there. Was it getting larger? Nahh… Couldn't be. Surely it wasn't turning blue, either.

She gave her head a firm shake, in case something might have rattled loose.

Still there.

Oh-kaayyy, she thought. Perhaps she had gotten a bit dehydrated, or maybe her blood sugar had plummeted without the normal feeling of nausea. Without taking her eyes

12

off of the growing ball of light, she reached over the top of the treadmill and snatched a peppermint candy from one cup-holder, her water bottle from the other.

She jumped back, startled, when suddenly the ball of light burst into a shower of sparkling bits of dust that ejected outward, hesitated in mid-flight, then submitted to the gentle pull of gravity.

And in the midst stood the shape of a person. A *man*, to be exact. A tall, lean, gorgeous man.

Wearing an orange satin suit.

Chapter Two

"Hello?"

Sebastian waved aside the last glittering particles of pixie dust and peered at the woman whose voice sounded like smooth bourbon. That she was a woman and not a child should have immediately set off warning bells in his head, but he was too absorbed with the view to be alarmed.

His gaze traveled quickly from her athletic-shoe clad feet, over shapely calves to well-toned thighs and gently flared hips clothed in cut-off sweat pants. Above the rolled-down waist of her shorts, her own narrow waist was bare, revealing a firm stomach—with a temptingly 'outie' belly button. Her smallish breasts were flattened against her chest by the sport bra she wore, which accentuated the broadness of her shoulders.

She was breathing hard, he realized, and his pulse leapt, until he realized she stood beside an immense tread-mill that still hummed slightly.

"Hello?" she said again, a twinge of impatience in her voice, and his gaze rose to her face. Her cheeks were flushed from exertion, her lips slightly apart as she breathed, making her look freshly fu——

What the hell was he doing? He jerked his gaze from her tempting lips to the wide gray eyes that looked directly at him. "Who are you?" he asked finally, annoyed with himself.

She raised an eyebrow. "I should ask you the same

question."

He chuckled incredulously. "I'm Sebastian Phate, your faerie guardian..." he hesitated. "Ehh, perhaps not *your* faerie guardian. I'm sure there's been some mistake." He patted his chest absently, then reached into the appropriate breast pocket of his blazer and pulled out the assignment paperwork. Opening it, he looked again at the name of his assignment. "Are you Kelsey Schroder?"

She nodded, making her blond ponytail bounce.

"Kelsey *Marie* Schroder?"

Again she nodded.

"Hmmm... Is this 561 Elmore Boulevard?"

"Yes."

"Born June twelfth, nineteen sev—" He gasped slightly. "Why you're 30 years old!"

"Thanks for reminding me."

"Obviously there's been a mistake. Faerie guardians are for disadvantaged children, not well-shaped women."

Her delicate eyebrows rose. "Pardon me?"

He cringed inwardly. "Well-*off*, I meant well-off."

"What makes you think I'm well-off?"

"I uh..." *Come on, Sebastian...* "I just assumed."

"Okay, who put you up to this? Was it Gina? Benji? Gerhardt? And how did you do that?"

"Ehh, excuse me?"

"You don't expect me to believe you're actually a fairy godmother, do you? Come on, who put you up to this?"

"Of course I'm not a fairy godmother," he informed her, rolling his eyes with disdain. "First of all, its 'faerie', with an 'ae' and an 'ie', not an 'ai' and a 'y'. Second of all, the politically correct term these days is the genderless 'guardian', not godmother or godfather."

"I see." She tapped her chin thoughtfully. "Does Elvis talk to you?"

"I fail to see what Elvis has to do wi—Ohhh." His eyes narrowed. "You're implying that I'm slightly off balance."

"Look, I don't mean to insult you, and truthfully I should be assessing my own mental stability, since I'm the one who thinks she saw a gorgeous man suddenly appear her bedroom. I just want to know why you're here."

He grinned. "Gorgeous?"

Her arms folded across her chest and she tilted her head at him in an entirely adorable way. "Why are you here?"

"I can't answer that question. I don't know. This is the assignment information I was given."

"Okay, then how did you do that—that—poofing thing with the glitter?"

"This?" he asked, then disappeared into a poof of glittering particles.

"Yes, that would be it."

"It's just part of the job," he said from behind her.

Kelsey spun around to see more pixie dust settling around him. "What happened to the dancing ball of light?"

"I only use that when I want to get a new client's attention."

Kelsey had a nagging suspicion that either he was exactly what he claimed to be, or she was losing her ever-loving mind. For the sake of expedience, she decided to go with the first option, no matter that choosing it might in fact support the second option. If he was anything like the fairy godparents on television, he could be a tremendous asset to her job. "Do you grant wishes?"

"Within reason—and within the law."

"Can I make one?"

"Sure, I suppose." He sighed heavily, no doubt expecting something extravagant.

"I wish for six cases of QuickRice."

His eyes widened in bewildered surprised. "*Rice?*"

"Rice."

Six cases of QuickRice appeared stacked in the far corner of her bedroom.

Kelsey smiled, deciding that having a fairy god—er…faerie guardian—could be a really good thing. Especially one who looked like that.

Where he stood now, the light from the bedside lamp reflected off the shiny fabric of his slacks in just such a way as to highlight an impressively sized bulge behind the zipper. Sheesh, if he was that big flaccid, she could only imagine how big he'd be fully erec—

Whoahhh Nellie! She had to find something else to concentrate on, like those large masculine hands with wide palms and long fingers—*No! Not a good idea.* Hmm… How about that god-awful suit?

Sebastian blinked, his mind suddenly blank. Whatever it was he'd been thinking about was gone, replaced by the sight of the hard points which suddenly jutted through the thin fabric of her sport bra. He felt a stirring in his loins and immediately looked at the carpet, turning his thoughts to boring tedious paperwork. New pony; filled. Barbie dream house; filled. Ohh, but she had a beautiful smile. Paperwork. All the money in the world; declined. Super Smasho drum set—

"So what's with the suit?"

His head jerked up. "Excuse me?"

"The suit. Is that like standard issue or something?" Her gaze drifted over him, lingering slightly below his belt.

"No, we're free to wear whatever we want, within reason of course."

"And *that's* within reason?"

"Are you insulting my suit?"

Her eyes grew even wider, as though she were surprised by her own audacity. "I'm—I'm so sorry," she said.

"I tell you I don't mean to insult you and then I insult you." She shook her head and sighed. "I'm a little out of sorts, maybe. I've never had a six foot man—"

"Six foot two."

"—appear out of thin air in my bedroom before, no matter how many times I wished it." She laughed apologetically. "I guess the orange satin was too much for my senses."

He ignored the suit jibe and focused on the statement before it. "You wished it?" Wishes were his area of expertise.

"I'm kidding. Well, no not really. I *have* wished that a million times, but, you know, never *seriously* expecting it to happen."

"Of course."

"Aren't you supposed to have wings and a wand?"

"We've not had wings for several centuries. And only the traditionalists carry a wand anymore."

"I see." She nodded slowly.

Sebastian grinned. He'd not had a real conversation with a fully human adult in a long time. In fact, he couldn't remember *ever* having a conversation with a fully human adult, because adults couldn't see him. So in theory he shouldn't be having this conversation. Which reminded him…

"I need to get back to headquarters. There must—"

"Ohhh no you don't." Kelsey stepped forward and grasped the lapels of his blazer, hoping he couldn't 'poof' while she had a hold on him. "It's been four years since there was a man in my bedroom. You're not leav…." The last word died on her tongue as she realized her mistake. She had pulled him closer, and now his divinely muscled chest was just inches from her lips. Her mouth went dry and her pulse went berserk. Without thinking, she flattened her palms against his chest, felt the firmness and

18

bulk beneath her fingers. Another mistake. "Um…" She looked up to find his golden eyes blazing. "I didn't mean that the way it sounded." Was that *her* voice so breathless? Her gaze fell to his lips, which were parted slightly, bearing the hint of a smile.

"Didn't you?" he asked, his voice generously laced with good humor.

"Um..." She couldn't quite remember the question, but she was pretty sure the answer was no, so she shook her head. "No."

She continued to gaze at his sensuous lips, unable to step away from him.

"Then how *did* you mean it?"

"Mean what?"

A low chuckle rumbled forth from his chest, bringing her back to her senses. She stepped back abruptly.

"I'm *so* sorry. I—I don't know what got into me."

Just when Sebastian was thinking that *he'd* like to get into her and that headquarters could wait, Kelsey thankfully made the right decision for him.

"You're right. There's probably another—younger—Kelsey Schroder out there who really needs a godparent. I'm sorry. I'm being selfish."

"Would you like another wish before I go?" he asked, his voice husky. Maybe she would wish for a wild roll in the sack.

"Really?"

"It's the least I can do."

She smiled warmly and thought for a fraction of a second. "I wish for…six dozen boxes of macaroni and cheese."

His heart sank. "Are you sure?"

No sooner had Kelsey nodded than a pile of mac-n-cheese boxes appeared beside the rice in the corner.

"Well, it was nice meeting you, Kelsey Schroder."

He tucked the paperwork back into the breast pocket, almost regretting his departure.

"Thank you, Sebastian."

He suppressed the delicious tremor that niggled his spine at the sound of his name on her lips. "Don't mention it." And then he disappeared before he changed his mind.

Chapter Three

Kelsey stood alone in the middle of her bedroom. The glittering dust that marked Sebastian's soundless departure settled slowly to the carpet, and as she watched, began to dissolve. She stared at the spot for long minutes, until there was no evidence at all that anything out of the ordinary had just occurred.

Had she somehow imagined it? Quickly she glanced into the corner, almost relieved to see that the boxes of rice and pasta were still there. But she walked over and picked up a box of macaroni and cheese anyway, just to make sure. Shaking it, she breathed a small sigh of relief. Maybe she wasn't totally losing her mind. If this stuff was still here after she got out of the shower, she'd feel that much better about the state of her sanity.

She set the box down and headed to the kitchen.

Faerie Guardian, huh? Who would have thought such beings really existed? And who would have thought they were so damned good looking, too? Kind of put the cute little old ladies she saw in the movies to shame.

She sighed, disappointed. It would have been nice to have a man—er… a Faerie Guardian—for a while.

She should have wished for him to fix the lock on her front door! Darn it!

Eh, the wishes she got were well spent.

She opened the refrigerator, hoping that something nutritious had somehow poofed into it, but no such luck, unless she wanted another protein bar.

She opened the freezer, but there was nothing appetizing in there, either.

Maybe she'd be hungrier after a shower—

She froze as her gaze fell on the blue envelope still on top of the stack of mail. The letter! And Sebastian!

She snatched up the letter and started to re-read it. But before she got to the end, it disappeared into a poof of powdery dust that got into her nose and made her sneeze.

Well...aaahhhh-choo! I guess they discovered their mistake. Perhaps Sebastian was even now introducing himself to the *correct* Kelsey Schroder.

She sighed, but didn't have much more time to ruminate on the subject, because her mobile phone rang.

"Are you watching the news?" Benji gushed without even a hello.

"No... Why?"

"Kirkpatrick is extolling the virtues of Wings and plugging the banquet."

"He is?"

"Yeah, it's so sweet it's almost nauseating."

Kelsey picked up the remote and turned the TV on. Sure enough, there was Mayor Bryce Kirkpatrick on Channel Five news, looking perfectly handsome and plastic. Blond hair, blue eyes, practiced smile. "If they were going to do a lead-up story on the banquet, why didn't they contact *us*?"

"You got me. My guess it was Kirkpatrick's idea. You know how he likes the limelight."

"Yeah." She did—it was a large contributing factor in why she had resisted his overtures over the last year or so. He was a nice guy, but a bit too showy for her tastes. She couldn't imagine that he would be a good kisser, either.

"He's such a cutie, Kels. You should give in and go

out with him."

"Uhh, thanks for the advice, Benj, but I'll pass. This is exactly why I won't ever be more than friends with him."

"I'll bet he did this for you."

"More like he did it to impress me with his media prowess. But there are far better things that impress me more."

Like warm golden eyes, an irresistible smile, and— Stop.

"Well, I just wanted to give you a heads up. See you tomorrow at the office."

"Thanks," she said, and hung up. On the television, a reporter introduced footage from last year's banquet. She'd had to veritably *plead* with the stations to get them to send a camera, and now there she was, in her trusty gray knit gown, shaking hands with the Mayor in front of a table of hors d'oeuvres.

She sat down on the couch and soon became engrossed in the rest of the news, then a rerun of *Friends*.

At eight o'clock, she trudged into her bathroom feeling utterly exhausted. She peeled off her clothes and reached into the shower to turn the water handle, then retreated until it got hot.

While she waited, she looked at herself in the mirror over the sink with a critical eye. Age was starting to creep up on her—which was a big reason she was almost religious about that treadmill. She wanted to be firm and youthful for a lot more years yet.

She leaned in to get a better look at the crow's feet starting at the corners of her eyes. That's what she got for smiling so much. Maybe by the time the wrinkles grew pronounced enough that they bothered her, she'd be able to afford Botox injections.

Pshhh. Who was she kidding? She'd probably never make much more than she did now. As Gina often pointed out, the morally fulfilling jobs never paid very much. If she wanted to live the high life, she should have signed on with a huge firm that liked to manipulate their accounts.

Kelsey shrugged at herself in the mirror. Bright orange jumpsuits weren't all that becoming. And she could only imagine what the other inmates would do to a homely book-cooking *accountant*. Sheesh.

Steam began to condense on the mirror and Kelsey realized the water was hot.

"Great. Wasted energy, bigger bills," she told herself as she stepped into the oblong shower cubicle. To make up for it, she hastily wet her hair, grabbed the shampoo, lathered and rinsed, then slathered on conditioner.

Reaching for her bath puff and shower gel, she took a short moment to inhale the fragrance with a contented sigh. This was one of the only luxuries she allowed herself. She loved the spicy floral scent, and reluctantly paid ten dollars a bottle for it at the bath shop in the mall. She'd been using the gel and lotion for nearly ten years; it was her signature scent. It made her feel exotic and sexy—at least for the few moments in the shower while she luxuriated in the fragrant bubbles.

With a smile, she worked the gel to a foam in her bath puff and began to scrub at her arms and legs.

Then she moved to her chest where the nylon mesh seemed to scrape over her aching nipples, sending bolts of electricity to her core and thoughts of a six-foot-two man in an orange satin suit to her head.

Mmmmm... She would have loved to get him out of that suit. She imagined him lying on her bed gloriously naked, his cock, thick and long, erect against his belly.

She stroked the bath puff over her belly and hips, then dipped it between her legs. Holding her labia open, she cleansed herself thoroughly from front to back, shivering as the puff brushed her clitoris, and again as it tickled her anus.

As the suds rinsed away, her fingers lingered in the closely shorn thatch of hair between her legs, stroking lightly over her clit. She was wound tight and could really use a good orgasm to release some of the tension. But she didn't want to stand here and waste more water, and she needed more than a quick rub—she needed substance. Her mind flew to the blue plastic box in the top of her closet—the one she brought down when she was feeling particularly horny. And she was feeling exceptionally horny right now. Though nothing in that box could truly be a substitute for the real thing—she thought briefly of a rather large bulge behind orange satin—but two or three of them used in tandem could certainly provide ample satisfaction.

Her hands now shaking, she carefully and quickly shaved and rinsed, then turned the water off and grabbed a towel. Hastily she dried and tucked the towel around her chest, then opened the bathroom door and started to dash to her closet. But instead, she jumped back in surprise.

"Oh dear mercy you startled me!"

Sebastian sat on her bed, hunched over with his elbows on his knees, looking at the carpet. His jacket lay neatly draped beside him. Which left him in a snug orange tank top that revealed deliciously bronzed shoulder muscles and impressive biceps. She gulped as her heart thundered. "I thought you were gone!"

"I was, but they sent me back," he groused, not looking at her. "They've started an investigation into the situation, but in the interim I'm to remain with you."

"Really? I thought—"

"I should know more tomorrow."

Whatever she might have said about the letter was forgotten in the wake of his acerbic tone. "Please don't curb your enthusiasm on my account." It was supposed to sound facetious rather than sardonic, but she couldn't hide the stab of irritation she felt. And perhaps it was tinged a bit with her own building frustration. She needed an orgasm, dammit! Instead of going to the closet as originally planned, she stalked to her dresser, turning her back to him.

"I didn't mean to insult you."

"No big deal. Now we're even." She shrugged and rummaged in her drawer, choosing a blue silk nightgown and looking for a pair of panties.

So what if he really didn't want to be here? Perhaps he'd seen the desperate hunger in her eyes and got scared. Perhaps he preferred younger women. Or perhaps Faerie Guardians just didn't experience the same physical desires regular humans did. So what?

Where the crap was a pair of panties? She normally preferred to wear thongs, little satin, lace, and string things, sort of her own way of feeling sexy even if no one ever knew, and that's the bulk of what was in her drawer. But she didn't know how long Sebastian would be staying. No need to risk accidentally mooning him. Especially since he was so grumbly about having to come back.

He touched her elbow, startling her yet again. She'd been so busy grousing and grumbling herself that she didn't realize he'd come to stand beside her. But now she could feel the heat from his body curl around her, and it made her cunt ache even more. And he could no doubt see all the lacy thongs in her underwear drawer! Heat crept up into her cheeks as she allowed him to turn her body to face him, but she couldn't meet his gaze.

"Kelsey."

She continued to look at the neckline of his orange shirt, and noticed how his pectorals created just a tiny bit of cleavage.

"In no way do I mean to imply that I have any less enthusiasm for this assignment than I do any other. It's

26

just highly irregular, and somewhat problematic."

That brought her head up. "Problematic?"

"First of all, I haven't the faintest idea how to go about being a faerie guardian for a grown woman. My experience is with kids."

She was unconvinced. "I see. And secondly?"

Now he finally glanced at the drawer she hadn't yet closed because she hadn't yet found any full-bottom panties. His eyes grew dark and he visibly gulped. "Secondly?"

Kelsey tried to pretend she had nothing to hide, and nodded expectantly.

"There is no secondly."

She rolled her eyes. "Why would you say 'First of all' if there is no 'Second of all'?"

"I don't know." But the pulse in his neck belied his words.

"Uh-huh." She raised a doubtful eyebrow. "If you'll excuse me, I probably ought to go get into my nightgown." Shaking her head, she grabbed the first pair of underwear she touched, not caring if it were panties or thong, slammed the drawer and tried to step around him.

But he stepped in front of her again, halting her in mid-step. "And secondly..."

Kelsey paused expectantly, looking up at him.

He rubbed the back of his neck and looked at the bed, then at the floor. "The truth is I... I have *too much* enthusiasm for this assignment—and that could be a problem."

Was he saying what she hoped he was saying? Was he really as horny as she was? Kelsey's heart skipped a beat, backed up, did a somersault, and started again at triple speed. But her brain issued a nasty caution: *He might be bluffing, trying to scare you.* Outwardly, she merely raised a contemplative eyebrow. "I see."

"Do you?" His voice sounded doubtful.

"I see that you're bluffing, trying to get me to send you away."

His eyes widened in affront. "*What*?"

"You're probably immune to that sort of 'enthusiasm' anyway. Look, if you want to go, *go*. Find a grade school Kelsey Schroder to take care of. I won't report you to the boss, or anything like—" She gasped as his kiss cut off her words.

Kelsey had been kissed a lot of times by a lot of men. In fact that's all she'd done with the vast majority of the men she'd dated. She had a theory that the way a man kissed revealed much about his personality and sexual prowess. She never fucked a man who couldn't kiss. So she found it odd, in this surreal moment while her brain tried to assimilate the power of his lips, that while she had imagined him naked and aroused, ready to relieve the ache between her thighs, she never once wondered if he would be a good kisser or not.

It would have been wasted time anyway, her brain decided as her lips parted and he delved inside, alternately suckling and cherishing her lips and tongue.

He wasn't a good kisser.

He was a *stellar* kisser.

And she felt the precursors of an orgasm as her soaring awareness rocketed back into her body, straight to her throbbing pussy. She grew lightheaded and fortunately remembered to breath. Because if she'd passed out, she would have missed her very first ever kiss-induced orgasm.

Stunned, she clung to him, milked his tongue and panted as the potent waves of pleasure washed over her.

Then she sagged against him.

Finally he ended the kiss and rested his forehead against hers. "Ms. Kelsey, I assure you I am not immune to that sort of enthusiasm."

A wicked smile tugged at the corner of her mouth.

"I'm not convinced." It came out sounding every bit the dare she intended it to be.

He sucked in a breath, no doubt as surprised as she at her boldness. For a moment he hesitated, as though debating with himself, and she thought he might pull away. Then he reached up and covered her hand with his own where it rested on his chest and slid it down to his rigid cock—his *large* rigid cock, every bit as thick and long as she'd imagined.

Now it was her turn to suck in a breath. Through the smooth satin of his slacks, she felt how very much his immunity was lacking. Her own needy body responded enthusiastically, instantly rushing lubrication to her delicate tissues in anticipation of a good hard fuck. *Oh please oh please oh please.*

He waited for her gaze to meet his, then with an answering dare in his eyes, released her hand, leaving it pressed against his cock.

Some semblance of sensible thought inched it's way to the front of her mind, a precious shred of reason amid crazy wanton lustful desires: She *should* pull away, satisfied that he was not, in fact, immune.

Satisfied? Her salacious mind snorted. *Nuh-uhh, honey.*

He groaned low in his throat and she realized she was stroking him.

Oh, she wanted satisfaction, all right, but simple knowledge that he did too wasn't gonna do it. She smiled and kissed the bare skin of his shoulder, nipping slightly with her teeth as her hand explored his length through his pants. Her other hand slid around to his back and tugged his shirt from his waistband, then trailed over the warm smooth skin of his back.

Sebastian squeezed his eyes shut and gritted his teeth, quickly losing control. Her soft wet mouth on his shoulder nearly drove him insane, and yet he couldn't help but imagine that mouth on his throbbing member, which now swelled painfully under her muted touch. His muscles bunched, his hands fisted, as he desperately tried to restrain himself from sweeping her up, plopping her on the bed, and hammering into her like a goddam caveman.

This was insane. He should not be reacting so swiftly and thoroughly to a woman. He needed to stop her before he lost his grip on the floodgates of passion that bulged as ominously as the front of his pants. "Kelsey, you should stop," he managed, his voice a gravelly croak.

Too late he realized how that must have sounded. He felt her head come up to look at him before she gasped and stepped back. His eyes snapped open as he tried unsuccessfully to prevent her retreat, and he instantly regretted his choice of words. Intense color rose swiftly to her face, her gray eyes wide with mortification.

Chapter Four

"I'm—I'm so sorry! I thought—"

"Kelsey, that's not what I meant—" He reached for her but she stepped back again

"I'm sorry—"

"*Don't* be sorry. Kelsey—Oh, fuck it." He took one large step, scooped her into his arms, and plopped her into the middle of the bed. The towel thankfully didn't make the trip and slid off the edge of the mattress, leaving her beautiful body bare to his hungry gaze. "How is it that I've known you all of three hours and all I can think about is having you wrapped around me in every way I can think of?" He asked this through gritted teeth as he pulled his shirt over his head with one hand and yanked open the fly of his slacks with the other, sending a button flying. The look of astonishment on her face lasted only a moment before her gaze fell to his generously-sized cock (if he did say so himself), which sprang eagerly and fully erect from his trousers.

"Has it only been three hours?" she asked breathlessly, tugging hard at her nipples and opening her legs. "Oh god, Sebastian, please hurry."

"One hundred eighty-nine minutes and thirty-seven seconds—but who's counting?" His eyes were drawn to the swollen pink cleft between her thighs and he groaned aloud. Moisture wept from her channel, creating a pearlescent dribble that disappeared between the cheeks of her ass. Unable to help himself, he dipped his mouth to catch the dribble with his tongue, lapping at the salty-sweet nectar of her body, raking his teeth gently over her engorged clitoris.

"Oh *god*, Sebastian!" she gasped, bucking her hips against his face. He slid his hands over the silky skin of her hips to hold her steady. The fingers of one of her hands tangled in his hair and she held his head against her as her other hand rolled and tugged her nipples. "Oh god oh god oh god!"

He inserted one finger, then two, into her sheath, and was pleasantly surprised to find she wasn't nearly as small as he thought she'd be.

Her hips lifted off the bed as she came suddenly and violently, thrashing and gasping for breath. It was all Sebastian could do to hold on and continue the work of his tongue, drinking her essence and restraining his own, until the initial tremors subsided.

Then he kissed his way hungrily up her twitching body, nibbling and suckling, unable to contain the low growl that emanated from his throat. He had to get inside her *now*, before he exploded onto the comforter. The tiny whimpering and mewling noises she made were only making him harder.

His mouth reached her lips and he lingered only a moment before he sat up, grasped her hips and surged inside with one not-so-gentle thrust, eliciting an impassioned cry from them both, hers laced with equal parts pain and pleasure. She was extremely tight, despite his earlier conclusion, her pussy hugging him like a velvet vice, still twitching from her recent orgasm. Embedded to the hilt, he could feel her inner walls stretching to accommodate him, so he held himself still, allowing her body a few small moments to adjust lest he ravage her.

He leaned down, holding her gaze, intending to take

a pebbled nipple into his mouth.

But he paused as an odd sensation washed over him. Time seemed to slow as a hot effervescence welled up in his chest, then languorously billowed out to his limbs, leaving a heavy hazy glow in its wake. He couldn't begin to explain it, but it nearly brought tears to his eyes.

He saw Kelsey's eyes go wide, her beautiful lips making a small "O", then her eyes closed and her back arched off the bed. Was she feeling it, too?

Slowly the effervescence faded from his limbs and drew back, coiling at his center, until his entire awareness was filled with his pulsing cock and the exquisitely tight walls that confined it. He closed his eyes and savored the intensity of the feeling, of the moment.

Then fingernails dug into his hips, urging him to move, so he did. His sensitive skin scraped over her inner walls, sending delicious shockwaves of pleasure shimmering through him. Again and again. Harder and harder.

Gradually his full senses returned, and he became aware of Kelsey's legs wrapped around him and her upthrust breasts as she arched urgently against him. Remembering his original intent, he bent his head to take a rigid nipple into his mouth.

She cried out as he suckled deeply on first one breast, then the other, using his teeth to nibble and tug.

"Harder," she pleaded, and he obliged, pounding his hips into her. She began to pant and buck once more, her orgasm imminent. He felt his own balls tighten, his stomach muscles clench as his own release gathered force. Seconds later, her inner muscles began to convulse around him as she screamed his name, and he erupted inside her with a roar.

He continued to thrust into her until her body stilled and his own spasming cock began to soften. Then he collapsed against her, all strength gone from his body, ejaculated in the most mind-blowing fuck he'd ever experienced.

Kelsey, too, was spent, breathing heavily. She couldn't remember *ever* having an orgasm so intense. She lay dazed for long minutes, enjoying the afterglow in her body, as well as the feel of Sebastian's weight on top of her, of his thick cock still imbedded in her.

She squeezed her inner muscles around him and he jerked slightly.

A low chuckle rumbled from his chest and he raised himself to look at her, a sleepy satisfied smile on his face. "I think I just gave you my entire life force."

"Mmm-hmmm, and it's leaking onto the comforter."

His eyebrow raised as he concentrated on the sensations around his penis. "Hmmm… maybe I can get some of it back."

He lifted himself from her and his cock slid out with a small slurping noise. She barely had time to notice that he was still somewhat hard before his mouth descended to her vulva once more and began lapping at their combined juices.

"Oohhhhh!" she gasped, surprised he would do such a thing. Surprised, but incredibly turned on. His tongue delved into her cunt, then withdrew to flutter against her clit, only to delve into her cunt again. "Oh, god, here I go again…" she whispered as her body began its ascent to the highest peaks.

"Here you *come* again," he rumbled into her pussy, the vibrations sending her over the edge.

"Sebastian!" she cried as she tumbled through yet another orgasm, then fluttered back to her body as surely as his tongue still fluttered over her clit.

When she could breathe again, she reached for him and pulled him up to kiss her. The taste of *them* on his lips made her smile. And the smile fostered a small giggle, which grew into an all-out laugh. She felt so utterly *satis-*

fied that she couldn't contain the bliss of her soul.

Sebastian lifted his head to look at her as she descended into a fit of joyous laughter. "Is it something I said?" he asked, a twinge of concern in his voice.

She shook her head and waited for the mirth to settle a bit before answering. "*That* was the most amazing sex I've ever had in my life!" She smacked the comforter for emphasis. "I am... I'm so... Oh! I don't have the words for it!"

"Is that a compliment?"

"Oh *god*, yes. I'm—I'm—speechless."

He lay back against the pillows. "Careful, you'll inflate my ego...among other things..."

Her gaze darted to his cock, which didn't seem to have diminished in size at all. It lay against his belly, long and rigid. Such wonderful things that thing could make her feel! "What was that warm bubbly feeling?"

"You felt it too?"

She propped herself up on one elbow and nodded. "It kind of suffused my body, making me tingly and warm all over, then coalesced into my cunt, making me *feel* every little nuance of your cock as you moved in me. What *was* that?"

"I have no idea. It's never happened to me before."

"You mean you didn't make it happen?"

"Not that I know of."

"Whatever it was... whew." She shook her head, at a loss for words.

They both lay in silence for a few moments more, letting the experience sink in.

"Did you say four years?" Sebastian rolled onto his side as he asked it, then pressed his lips to her forehead.

"Uh-huh."

"Why so long?"

"I don't know. Lack of time? Aversion to mediocrity? Complacency? Lots of reasons, I guess."

"No one appeared in your bedroom and had his way with you?"

"Unfortunately not, as that seems to be very effective." Kelsey traced the circumference of his nipple. "Of course now you're thinking I'm a sex-starved hussy."

His eyes twinkled and he let his gaze rake meaningfully over her naked body, then glanced at his open pants and renewed erection. "Aren't you?

"Maybe a little…" she admitted with a sheepish smile.

They settled into a comfortable silence, which seemed somewhat odd to Kelsey. Weren't comfortable silences reserved for established relationships? Why did she feel so totally comfortable with this man? Was it magic? Karma? Fate? Wasn't that his last name?

A rumbly gurgling sound broke the quiet.

"Is that your stomach?"

Kelsey grinned self-consciously. "Yeah. I've only eaten a protein bar since lunch."

"Would you like to wish for some dinner?"

"Nah. I've got food in the freezer. You hungry?"

He raised an eyebrow. "Is that a trick question?"

She laughed and sat up, reaching for the robe draped over the footboard. "Come on. I need to eat even if you don't."

In the kitchen, she dug a bag of frozen shrimp and veggies out of the freezer while Sebastian took a seat in the dining room. She dumped the bag into a skillet and looked at him through the pass-through. "So what does remaining with me entail—besides hot sex?"

He leaned back in his chair, eyes twinkling as he watched her stir the food and adjust the heat under it. "That wasn't exactly in the job description."

"I imagine not—Oh!" A terrible thought occurred to her. "You're not going to get in trouble for it, are you?"

He shook his head. "Guardians are loosely bound by a generous code of ethics, and usually by the laws of the land."

"And in lay terms that means…?"

He shrugged. "We're allowed to bend the rules when necessary."

"Well… feel free to indulge further." Had she actually said that out loud? Dear mercy where had this wanton woman come from?

Sebastian nodded. "Just say the word."

Now! Kelsey thought, fighting the urge to unzip his pants again and straddle him in the chair. He was hard for her again, she knew, a thought that gave her an outrageously sexy thrill. Unfortunately she really needed to eat, so stayed at her post by the stove, stirring the mixture to keep it from burning.

"I've never played host to a fai—faerie guardian before. I obviously don't know what you need or require."

"We don't require anything—we provide for ourselves." His eyebrows raised as his golden eyes grew heavy and seductive. "*Need*, as you might guess, is an entirely different matter."

Her body tingled under that needy gaze. She took a calming breath and redirected the conversation. "Do you sleep?"

"Only if there's nothing else to do." He grinned.

When the shrimp and veggies were heated through, she served up two plates and brought them to the table. As she sat eating, exhaustion again settled on her shoulders, and she felt her eyes closing involuntarily. *Wake up, Kels.* She shook her head, but it was useless. Three orgasms was two more than she'd had in a looooong time—probably ever, and her body was drained.

Even still, after she'd cleared the dishes and crawled back into bed, Kelsey tried to keep her eyes open. She *really* wanted to indulge in another round of Sebastian's brand of sex—she didn't care how sore she'd be tomorrow, and she knew he was ready and willing. But hard as she tried, she couldn't keep her sated body from propelling itself toward dreamland. So, wrapped in his arms with his hard cock nestled between the cheeks of her bottom, she plunged into deep—and no doubt drooling—sleep.

Chapter Five

Kelsey emerged from her bathroom fully dressed, much to Sebastian's disappointment. She'd been in the shower when he woke, so he had lingered in her bed, hoping to lure her back for a quick romp to relieve the rock between his legs. He'd suffered most of the night until he'd given in and finally slid himself into her hot sheath. But not full-out fucking her had nearly killed him, especially when that warm, vaguely bubbling feeling had washed over him again, and she had groaned and writhed in her sleep.

Unfortunately she hadn't awakened, though, so he'd grit his teeth and endured until he'd finally fallen asleep.

Now she was no longer naked, dammit. But she looked damned good anyway. He watched her cross to her dresser, not bothering to hide the blatant appreciation in his gaze.

She wore a silky skirt that gently hugged her hips and flared into feminine ruffles below her knees. On top, she wore a simple baby blue scoop-neck long-sleeved t-shirt. Navy-blue sling-backs graced her feet, and her straight blond hair fell freely about her shoulders, already mostly dry.

"I need to leave here in twenty minutes," she said, putting an earring in her ear. "You're welcome to come with me if you'd like."

"I'd love to come with you…" he said in a deep sultry voice, unable to resist, "…and in you…and for you…and on you…but you're a bit overdressed at the moment."

She grinned and glanced at the tented sheet at his mid-section. "Let me rephrase that—for now. You're welcome to *accompany* me if you'd like."

"I'm sure I can find a way to do both."

"I'm counting on it. Now get up—er… get out of bed and get dressed if you're com—accompanying me to work."

"Yes, ma'am," he said and got out of the bed. He didn't miss her hungry gaze on his jutting cock as he made his way to the bathroom.

Ten minutes later, she pressed her lips together and eyed him with a pained expression.

"Is that what you're going to wear?"

He looked down at himself. "What's the matter now?"

"How do I say this gently? Um… Well…You look like a four-year-old picked your clothes for you."

Smoothing a hand over the chartreuse satin of his blazer, he lifted his chin indignantly. "I'll overlook the insult, primarily because my style sense appeals to my normal clientele. Besides, nobody else can see me, so I can't embarrass you any more than I already have."

"Are you sure nobody else can see you?"

"I'm only visible to my charge. That would be you."

She sighed. "I'm gonna trust you on that. Normal grown men do not wear lime green suits."

"It's chartreuse."

"Okay, and straight men call it lime green—Never mind. Sebastian?"

"Hmmm?"

"Can you help me carry these to my truck?" She gestured to the boxes of food in the corner.

"Sure. Where are you taking them?"

Kelsey considered just *wishing* them to her truck, but decided against it. Better to save her wishes for important things. So she stooped and picked up as much as she could carry whilst also juggling her purse and keys. "I'm taking them into work with me."

"Ah." Dutifully he picked up an armload—which was everything that remained—and followed her out the front door, somehow closing it behind him.

Outside, he stopped and gaped at the truck in her driveway with obvious scorn. "Is this your vehicle?"

She ignored the disdain in his voice and lifted her armload over the tailgate of her aging pick-up. "Hey, it runs. I don't care what it looks like as long as it gets me where I want to go." It was a small lie—she *did* care what it looked like, but there wasn't much she could do to make the twenty-year-old truck look like anything more than a twenty-year-old truck.

"I'll bet it guzzles gas." He set the rest of the boxes in the back.

"Yep, and oil, too. But it's all I've got. Are you trying to make up for the suit comments?"

He shrugged and cast a guilty look at the ground, a small smile on his lips. "Maybe."

She could only laugh. "Okay, let's call a truce. I'll try to ignore your clothes, and you try to ignore my truck. Deal?"

"Ignore my clothes?" His eyebrows wriggled as he grinned at her. "I like the sound of that."

Ordinarily such blatant sexual overtures would annoy the hell out of her, but somehow Sebastian managed to make them playfully sexy—and incredibly arousing. "Of course you do." And of course she imagined him naked—which is just what he wanted her to do. Fresh out of bed, hair mussed, cock hard and erect…she suppressed a shiver.

"Get in," she said, her mind now drawn to the pleasant chafing between her legs. Lord, she didn't know how she was going to get through the day without dragging him into the supply closet.

Several stoplights, a short jaunt on the freeway, and quick stop at Java Joe's later, they pulled into a parking lot outside a small brick building bearing a sign that read "Sophie's Wings Community Assistance."

Her father's legacy.

"A-ha. It makes sense to me now."

"What makes sense?" She turned the truck off and got out, glancing around to see if anyone were there to witness her seeming to talk to thin air. Thankfully the lot was empty except for a few cars.

He followed her out of the truck and closed his door. "The rice and macaroni. You work at a food bank."

"That information isn't in your file?"

"No, actually. There's no space for 'workplace' anymore because kids don't have one."

Just then an old man rode by on a bicycle. Even though he didn't slow or stop, his head swiveled to look at them as he passed. Vague dread crept over her.

"Okay, you're sure nobody else can see you?" she asked, not moving her lips.

"Positive."

When the old man had disappeared from sight, she motioned for him to follow her up the steps and entered the building, casually holding the door for him while trying not to look like she was holding the door. She continued down the hall as though she were alone, and smiled at the woman who stepped out of a nearby office.

"Good morning, Ellen."

"Hi Kelsey. Wow, that's *some* suit."

Both Kelsey and Sebastian stopped in their tracks as Ellen continued on out the door. Kelsey glanced at

42

Sebastian, who looked like he'd accidentally swallowed a bee.

"She could see me."

"I think the guy outside could, too."

"Adults aren't supposed to be able to see me."

"Sshhh. Well I can see you, and I'm an adult."

"But you're my charge. Of course you can see me."

"Perhaps if one adult can see you, all adults can see you."

"I wonder if kids can see me then?"

"Lots of little ones come through here with their moms each day, so you'll know soon enough. Come on." She needed to get him out of sight fast, so she quickly led him down the hall, past half a dozen more open doorways, to her own office.

"Executive Director?" Sebastian indicated the nameplate on the wall to the left of her door.

"Yeah…" She circled the desk and put her purse in the bottom drawer, then began sifting through the stack of messages on her desk. "Sort of by default. My dad founded Sophie's Wings when I was five. Sophie was my mom."

"Was?"

"She died when I was four. We were hit by a drunk driver and she was killed instantly. My dad never really got over that."

"I'm sorry."

She shrugged and gave a wistful smile. "I don't remember the accident, and I barely remember her. Just sort of a vague impression of sunlight and smiles. Most of my 'memories' are ones I got secondhand through my dad."

She continued to sort through messages as Sebastian walked around, looking at the certificates and photos on her walls. After reading all the messages—tossing one from Bryce Kirkpatrick in the trash, she cleared the top of her desk and sat down. Sebastian took one of the client chairs.

"Where's your dad now?" he asked, his voice moderately curious.

Thankfully a young man passing by in the hallway caught her attention, saving her from answering right now. "Oh! José! José?"

The summoned man poked his head in the doorway, glanced at Sebastian and looked back to Kelsey with a grin.

Kelsey pretended not to notice. "I'm so glad you're here! Are you headed back to the warehouse?"

He nodded, his warm brown eyes sparkling with contained mirth.

"Oh good. There's a load of food donations in the back of my truck. Could you take those with you, please?"

"Sure thing, missus. Consider it done." He gave a small salute, then continued down the hall, his chuckles echoing quietly off the walls.

Before she could offer Sebastian a mortified look, another man poked his head into her office.

"Hey Kelsey, did you see that guy in the chartreu— Oh, I—I'm sorry. I didn't realize he was with you."

"Hi Benji. Meet my friend Sebastian. He um... he works with kids a lot, so his wardrobe is supposed to appeal more to a much younger crowd."

"Oh really? You work with kids? What do you do?"

Sebastian's eyes grew wide. "I'm, uh... I'm a uh... I'm a counselor...at a youth center... in Saint Louis."

Benji gave him an odd look, then turned back to Kelsey, his eyes questioning.

Kelsey nodded. "You'll have to excuse him, his allergies were making him miserable this morning, so I gave him one of my allergy pills. He's a little muzzy still."

"Ah... Must be that mountain cedar. Gets me every year, too. I get allergy shots or I'd be completely out of commission every spring."

Sebastian dutifully snuffled and rubbed his eyes. "Whatever it is, it's kicking my bum."

"Bum… That's cute. Well I gotta go. Catch ya later, Kels."

When Benji left, Kelsey let her head drop to her desk. "That was rather embarrassing," she said into the blotter.

"If I'd known—"

She sat up and took a deep breath. "It's okay. We'll just hope the fashion police don't happen by."

After a beat, Sebastian leaned across the desk. "I could make it up to you," he said, his voice seductively soft.

Kelsey's eyebrow rose and she leaned closer, letting the neckline of her blouse gape a bit. "Oh? How so?"

He smiled a sexy little smile and opened his mouth to answer, but whatever he had in mind was preempted by the sound of a beeper going off. Both snapped to attention and checked the devices at their hips.

Too late, Kelsey realized she no longer *wore* a beeper since getting a mobile phone several years ago. *Old habits die hard.* But that didn't prevent her from feeling silly.

Sebastian looked at his beeper and sighed. "I'll be back in a bit," he said, then leaned over the desk to give her a kiss. A small taste and a nibble, and then he disappeared into a poof of pixie dust.

Kelsey's heart fell and she sighed deeply. She had hoped his superiors would take longer to figure out the mix-up. If Sebastian came back, it would no doubt be to say goodbye. Belatedly, she looked up at the door to make sure it was still closed, so that no one had seen a six-foot man apparently disappear into thin air.

"Well, I guess I've got work to do," she said to no one in particular as she picked up the remaining messages from the corner of her desk and reached for the phone.

Two and a half hours later, Kelsey finally hung up the phone. Lord knew she spent at least half her day on the phone, organizing donations and contributions, man-hours and disbursements. And she always made a mess of her desk, too. Not only did she have a habit of doodling on her blotter, but she frequently had to refer to client files, so they tended to pile up on the surface of her desk. She now had a stack several inches high.

With a sigh, she stood, picked up the folders and turned to the cabinet behind her desk.

The pleasant chafing sensation from earlier was now gone, but the area remained sensitized. She found herself swaying unnecessarily as she opened drawer after drawer and put the files in their places, enjoying the feather-light caress of her underwear against her skin. It reminded her of Sebastian's fluttering tongue.

"Pleasant thoughts?"

Kelsey's eyes, which she hadn't realized she'd closed, snapped open in surprise. Sebastian sat on the edge of her desk, pixie dust settling around him. She felt her cheeks grow even hotter. After stuffing the last file into place, she slammed the drawer shut and cleared her throat. "Back so soon?" she asked, a slight bristle in her voice at being caught.

He laughed, a low, sexy sound. "I'll take that as a yes."

"I may or may not have been thinking about you, though."

"Of course." He glanced at her blotter, which to her horror, had his name doodled over and over across it.

She propped a hip on the corner of her desk, using her body to shield his view of the drawings, hoping he'd missed the doodle of a gargantuan penis. "So did they get it figured out?"

He grinned. "Yes and no."

"Yes and no?"

"There was no mistake made. I've truly been assigned to you."

That made Kelsey grin, too. If she knew anything about bureaucracy, that meant the mistake was higher up in the ranks, and it could take *weeks* to find the source.

"They just don't know why. They haven't found the originating request to see who signed it."

"What's an originating request?"

"Sort of a work order. Only the higher-ups can issue them."

"Ah. So you're here for a while then?" Her heart leapt.

"Seems so. Until they get the paperwork straightened out."

"Then we really need to take care of a few things…"

"Such as…?"

"I wish for a hundred dollars."

He smiled as he reached into this pocket and pulled out four fifty-dollar bills.

"But this is two hundred."

"I know. I'm feeling generous—sort of as an apology for embarrassing you."

She was almost disappointed. "This isn't how you're going to make it up to me, is it?" Her bottom lip poked out.

He smiled. "Apology is different from atonement." His eyebrows waggled.

"Good, 'cause it's for you anyway." She grabbed her purse. "Let's go. We've only got forty-five minutes." She grabbed his warm hand, ignored the small current of electricity that seemed to flow up her arm, and led him down the hallway.

"For me? I don't need money."

"You do if you want to buy new clothes."

"I beg your pardon! I don't need new clothes! My wardrobe is perfect for younger—" He felt a tug on the hem of his blazer and looked down to see a pink-cheeked, pig-tailed little girl. "Yes?"

"Can you make me a gawaff?"

He smiled, not quite understanding her question. "A 'gawaff'?'"

"Hanna Leann!" The girl's mother rushed out of a nearby office. "I'm so sorry, sir. She's a little confused, I think." As Sebastian stood helplessly confused, the woman took the child's hand and led her back into the office. "I don't think he makes balloon animals, sweet pea."

He winced.

"A fwower?" Hanna asked her mother.

"I don't think so, baby. Here. Why don't you look at this book?"

"You were saying…?" Kelsey crossed her arms over her chest and pegged him with an 'I told you so' look.

He sighed. "All right. Let's go shopping."

* * *

"Wait here," Kelsey said, and pointed to one of three small upholstered chairs in the dressing room. "I'm gonna go find someone who works here. Do you know what size you wear?"

Sebastian searched his mind, looking for the information she requested. Then he shook his head. "No. I've always used magic to make my clothes."

"Okay, then I'll find someone with a measuring tape." She disappeared into the store.

Alone, he glanced at the tiny overstuffed chairs, and could just imagine himself sitting in one—knees at his chin, his back hunched as he tried to get comfortable. *Nah*. So he looked around instead. They were in the men's department at JCPenneys. Kelsey had brought him directly to the dressing room, as though she were embarrassed to be seen in public with him. Was his green suit really that bad?

He noticed that the room was sort of 'C' shaped, except with the hallways in straight lines instead of curved. He stood in the bottom of the 'C', where the overstuffed chairs squatted, waiting for weary dressers.

He followed the room back into a wide hallway, where smaller booths clustered on either side. Peeking in one, he immediately thought it was just the right size for a quick fuck. *Hmm...*

He continued down the wide hall until it turned right again, where there were more dressing booths—and a wall of angled mirrors at the other end.

Hot damn, he thought, going to stand in the middle of the mirrors. Forget the booths. He wanted to fuck Kelsey *here*, where he could watch from a myriad of angles. He imagined her palms pressed against the glass, her face a mask of ecstasy, her breasts bouncing from a million different angles, as he pounded into her from behind. He groaned as his dick tightened painfully.

Distraction... He sighed and walked down the hallway and back, looked at the dozen or so pictures on the wall. Men wearing blue jeans and khakis, shorts, slacks... And not a chartr—lime green—garment among them.

"He's in here... Sebastian?"

He turned at the sound of Kelsey's voice. "I'm back here."

Kelsey appeared around the corner, followed by a young dark-haired woman.

"Oh dear," the younger woman said when she saw him. She exchanged glances with Kelsey.

"Excuse me. I *am* standing here, and I *can* see that look. Can we please get on with this?"

Kelsey glanced at her watch. "Oh, yes! We need to hurry. Sebastian, this is Tina. She's going to help find you some new clothes."

"You know what? It's kinda hard to get a look at your skin coloring with all that green. Could you take your jacket and shirt off? I can bring you a robe if you want."

No one could ever accuse him of being modest, but he suppressed a smile at the sly grin on Tina's face as he immediately shrugged out of his blazer, then peeled off his shirt. Both women no doubt noticed the erection he could feel jutting against the waistband of his slacks.

He glanced at Kelsey, whose eyes had gone dark. As he watched, the tip of her tongue darted out to moisten her bottom lip. He flexed his chest muscles and both women sighed.

He chuckled aloud.

"Oh-kay!" Tina snapped back to attention, her cheeks staining slightly. "Let me get you measured." She drew a measuring tape from her pocket. "Put your arms out, please."

Sebastian obeyed, following her directions while she measured his arms, chest, waist, and neck. Her face turned bright red as she very quickly measured his inseam.

"I'll be right back," she said, then disappeared down the short hallway.

When she had gone, Sebastian grabbed Kelsey's hand and pulled her into the nook of mirrors. "I want to fuck you right here, right now," he growled as he pressed her against the glass, his hard length nudging into her belly.

Her eyes glazed over and she sighed briefly. He could tell she was considering it, but then her eyes cleared and she smiled teasingly. "And here I thought it was Tina's hands all over you that had you all worked up. I should have known it was the mirrors."

"It was the thought of seeing you in the mirrors, seeing your face as I slide in and out of your tight, wet pussy."

She shivered on another sigh, a faint growl of her own rumbling from her chest.

"I have a bunch of— Oh. Umm… Sorry."

Sebastian turned his head without releasing Kelsey. Tina stood with an armload of clothes, so he reluctantly stepped back. "No problem. We were just… talking."

"Uh-huh. Well I brought a bunch of stuff for you to try on. I didn't know what style you'd like, so I brought a little of everything."

"Thanks, Tina." Kelsey stepped forward and took some of the clothes from the other woman's arms. "Sebastian, grab a few pair of these jeans and take them into that room to try them on." She pointed to the nearest booth.

"Help me?" he asked hopefully, taking the jeans from her.

"Nice try. Come on… We don't have much time. I have to be at a meeting in thirty minutes."

Obediently, he took the jeans and went into the changing room alone.

Fifteen minutes later, he stood with his back to the mirrors while Kelsey adjusted his collar. "There," she said, then stepped back to get the full effect. "Oh my god."

"What?" He glanced down at himself self-consciously, then turned to examine himself in the mirror. Did the black jeans and gray silk shirt make him look too severe? "What's the matter?"

Tina rounded the corner just then. "I found a pair of—Oh wow." She stopped in her tracks as her mouth dropped open.

"What?!" He turned around to look at them directly.

"Um, Sebastian?" Kelsey's voice seemed a bit breathless.

"Yes?!"

"You are um... You're—oh my god. You are so blazing sexy."

One eyebrow shot up. "Seriously?" A smile tugged at his lips.

Both women nodded.

Sebastian noted the sudden flush of Kelsey's cheeks, the increased rise and fall of her chest. She shifted her weight from one foot to the other and then back again. He waggled his eyebrow at her and tilted his head toward the mirrors. She bit her lip.

"I—I found a pair of boots that I thought would go well with all the stuff he chose." Tina set three boxes on the floor. "I brought three sizes, and socks, too."

"Thanks Tina, I appreciate your help."

"Just—leave what you're not buying here. I'll take care of it later." Apparently skittish all of the sudden, the younger woman wrung her hands for a few seconds, then left without another word.

When she was gone, Sebastian pulled Kelsey into his arms. "Do you think she'll call security if she hears us fucking?"

She smiled and pressed her lips to the bare skin at the vee of his shirt. "No time to find out. We've really got to go. It's just across the street, so I might even make it on time if there's no line at the checkout."

"Damn."

She pointed to the three boxes of boots. "Find a size that fits you while I clean up this mess."

Sebastian left the store with a monstrous hard-on, trying hard not to pout. It wasn't often that he didn't get his way. Unfortunately stopping time was beyond his capabilities, so he had to let Kelsey keep her appointment.

Chapter Six

Sebastian sat patiently in the small waiting area while Kelsey visited with an executive from Palmer Foods, one of Sophie's Wings' corporate donors. An outdated issue of *People* magazine lay open in his lap. He'd lost interest in it a while ago, but it still served to hide the unmistakable rod in his jeans. Right now a dangling sling-back shoe held his attention.

He could see her through the glass doors of the conference room, sitting daintily, legs crossed at the knees, shoe dangling from her bouncing top leg. She was attempting to go over some paperwork with a portly man in an expensive, yet ill-fitting suit. The man's gaze kept drifting to her legs while Sebastian tried to ignore an annoying niggle of jealousy. Temporary assignment, pleasant diversion, itch-scratching and all that, he reminded himself. But he *could* make the guy's suit shrink a size… Or make his chair tip over… Or his pen could burst and spray ink across his chest. Yeah… That would——

"Damn, you do look nice in normal clothes."

Sebastian looked up, startled to see Kelsey standing next to him. Perhaps he should have been paying less attention to Eyeballs and taken notice that the meeting was apparently over. Then her words registered in his brain, as did the flush of her cheeks and the appreciative hunger in her eyes. His heartbeat kicked up a few notches. "Thanks." Looking at him really made her hot? Maybe the chartr——

lime green suit had been a bad idea after all.

Kelsey's own pulse leapt as she watched him set the magazine back on the cocktail table and stand. Oh sheesh. *Cock*tail table. God he was *still* hard? She reluctantly tore her gaze away from his crotch as they made their way to the bank of elevators. "Sorry that took so long," she said, a little too breathlessly.

"He seemed to have a hard time concentrating."

"You noticed that, too?"

Sebastian nodded and pressed the down button to call the elevator.

She sighed. "Normally the Resource Director handles all this stuff, but Eugenia retired a few weeks ago. I guess I'm just not as effective or something. I had to repeat myself several times. I don't know where his mind was."

"I do."

"Oh?"

"Same place mine is."

The elevator doors opened with a ding and they stepped inside the empty car.

She pushed the 'Ground Floor' button, the doors soughed closed, and the elevator began its descent. "And where is that?" As if she had to ask!

"In your panties."

Suddenly the lights flickered, then went out completely as the elevator ground to a halt. Within seconds, a small yellow backup light came on, dimly illuminating the small enclosure.

"What's happening?"

"Minor elevator malfunction. They'll have it fixed in about fifteen minutes."

"Did you—?"

He nodded as he purposefully maneuvered her against the wall.

"Sebastian, I'm kind of claustrophohhhhhh..." He

pulled her hips against him, pressing his rigid manhood into her belly as his teeth raked her neck. She forgot what she was saying.

"I think I can keep you distracted," he whispered hotly before claiming her mouth. She was so tightly wound from the dressing-room overtures that she melted against him immediately, opening her lips to invite his tongue and winding her arms around his neck.

After searing her nerves with his kiss, his mouth drifted down her neck, nibbling at the tender skin under her ear. "Did you notice on the way up that these walls are mirrored?" he rumbled.

She hadn't noticed, but she couldn't find her voice to tell him so. She could only run hungry hands over the smooth silk of his shirt, feeling the hard muscles underneath.

He stepped back slightly, pulling her with him. Then gruffly, he turned her around, bent her forward, placed one of her hands against the wall of the elevator and held it there with his own. As he nuzzled her neck and grazed his teeth over her shoulder, his other hand hauled her skirt up to her waist.

"Sebastian." His name was a sigh on her lips, and it was all the encouragement he needed.

She moaned as he slid his hand over the bare skin of her bottom and squeezed. He loved the feel of her ass, the firm muscle covered with softness and silky smooth skin. And it pleased him that she wore such skimpy underwear. How very accessible it made her. He now pulled up the t-back of her thong, causing it so dig in and rasp against her anus, eliciting an even louder moan. He could smell the spicy scent of her passion, and a quick dip of his fingers between her legs confirmed that she was drenched.

"Have you ever fucked in an elevator, Kelsey?"

She shook her head, her heated gaze meeting his in

the reflective wall. "Not yet," she whispered sexily, arching her back slightly and lifting her hips against him.

His cock jerked and swelled even more inside his new jeans, and he wasted no time setting himself free. Released, his dick fell heavily against her ass, the head nudging her anus, and he briefly wondered if she'd ever been taken that way. But that wasn't on his agenda at the moment. He guided himself lower with his free hand.

"Stand on your tip-toes, love," he said as he tugged the crotch of her thong aside. She obeyed, and he spread his legs wide, crouching slightly until he was low enough to plunge his aching cock into her wet sheath.

She sucked in a breath, then let it out on a long moan as he began to thrust into her. "Yesssss…Oh, Sebastian."

"Sweet saints," he hissed out as a hint of last night's effervescent glow washed over him, nearly taking his breath away. "You feel so damned *good*."

"Ohhhhhh… Feels so good."

In their reflection, he watched the nuances of passion and pleasure cross her face as he increased his pace, soon slamming so hard and deep that he lifted her off her feet with each forward motion. His free hand tweaked a pebbled nipple through her t-shirt, then moved down to find her clitoris.

She ground her hips against him, rocking her pelvis in rhythm with his stroking fingers and plundering cock. Within minutes her body was quaking in his arms, her internal muscles pulling him to his own explosive release, as they both bit back their cries of passion. Pulse after pulse, he jetted endlessly into her, until they were both gasping.

He held her for long moments, supporting both of them with one hand braced against the wall as they struggled to catch their breath. Kelsey would have crumpled to the floor if not for still being impaled on his cock.

"Ohgodthatwasgood," she said on a roughly exhaled breath. "I can't believe we did that."

"Mmmmmm…" He flexed himself inside her as he kissed her neck. "We'll have to do it again sometime."

"Mmmmm…" she answered with a sated nod.

Reluctantly he withdrew from the velvety warmth of her body, the action making a slight slurping sound and sending juices dripping down her leg. "Eh…" he said. "Don't move."

After making sure she wouldn't wobble, he quickly put himself back together, then turned her to face him as he knelt in front of her.

"Wha—?"

He licked their combined juices from her thigh with a hum of pleasure. There was something indescribably erotic about the taste of *them*, of their intermingled essences.

"Oh god Sebastian, that is so hot." Her voice was tight and breathless, her small hands curling into his shoulders.

He grinned against her pussy, then delved his tongue into her folds to find more honey. Her hips tilted into his probing mouth. Harder he licked, sucking and lapping. Her hips rocked against him, and she moaned long and low.

Now he zeroed in on her clitoris, using his lips to isolate it, then nibbled gently with his teeth and soothed with this tongue.

Her hands held his head, crushing his mouth into her cunt, until she was moaning and gasping. "Oh god Sebastian!" she cried, falling violently over the edge of ecstasy into an orgasm he suspected was long and fierce. "Ohhhhhgoooooooddddd!"

The elevator flickered back to life as her body quieted, and they started moving again. He replaced the crotch of her thong, then sat back on his heels and let her skirt fall.

She clutched the railing, gasping. "I'll have to find more excuses... to be on the upper floors... of tall buildings." Her eyes twinkled with mischievous anticipation and she regained her breath.

"I'm sure I can help you think of some." He kissed her, letting her taste their essences.

He broke the kiss when the elevator doors opened, and two maintenance workers stared at them.

"You folks okay?" one of them asked.

"Fine now, thank you." Kelsey smoothed her hands over her skirt, making sure it was hanging as it should.

"My friend is a little claustrophobic, so she did get a little nervous, but I think I managed to keep her calm."

Both workers eyed her dubiously. They could no doubt smell the aroma of passion, since it was leaking down her leg despite Sebastian's erotic ministrations.

"Claustrophobic, huh?"

She nodded, knowing her cheeks were flaming.

"You gentlemen going down?" Sebastian asked as he laid a finger over the 'Door Close' button.

"Nope."

"Bye, then." The doors closed and the elevator car continued down three more floors to the lobby.

"I uh... I need to make a potty stop," Kelsey said as she dashed for the ladies room.

"You okay?"

"Yeah, fine. Feel a little *squishy* is all."

He laughed as the door swung closed.

When she returned to the lobby, he was propped against the huge pot of an indoor palm tree looking sated and sexy. The appreciative gazes of other women as they passed showed that Kelsey wasn't the only one who thought so. She felt a small thrill that such a gorgeous specimen of the male species was waiting for *her*.

He grinned as she approached. "Feel better?" he asked innocently, then pulled her into his arms for a quick kiss. Kelsey heard a few jealous sighs and almost giggled.

"Definitely less squishy."

"So what's next on the agenda?"

"Well, I forgot to grab the leftovers out of the fridge this morning, so we'll need to stop someplace for lunch, and then I have a new client meeting me at the office at one o'clock."

"Sounds good."

After they had stopped quickly at Subway, Kelsey turned to look at her companion when they were on the road again. If she met him on the street, she would never guess he spent his life catering to the whims of kids. Given his voracious sexual appetite, she wondered if he had much free time, or if he was a closet nympho like her.

"What's your personal life like, Sebastian?"

"What do you mean?"

"Well you apparently know your way around the bed-room—"

"—And the elevator," he supplied.

"—And the elevator," she agreed, shivering slightly. "So I'm presuming you have a personal life apart from your normal duties."

Sebastian laughed, ridiculously pleased that she wondered about his life. "Uh…yeah. For obvious reasons, I've never before encountered such temptation in my normal duties." He grinned, then shrugged. "I do occasionally date other Guardians, maybe once every decade or so."

"Once every *decade* or so? Sheesh, you're worse than I am. How old are you, anyway?"

"That's kind of a tough question, 'cause I'm not real sure. Guardian age is measured in assignments, not years, 'cause we don't really *have* years."

"Hmm." Her brow furrowed as she tried to understand, but then she blinked and visibly let it go. "Are there Guardian Singles Bars or something where you go to meet other Guardian singles?" she asked jokingly.

"Yes."

"Really?" She turned her head, her gray eyes alight with astonished amusement.

"Really." He shrugged again. "But my kind of woman doesn't hang out at singles bars."

"Where does your kind of woman hang out?"

"I don't know. She probably doesn't have time to hang out anywhere."

Just then Kelsey's mobile phone rang. She stuck the hands-free earpiece into her ear while she quickly swallowed her bite of sandwich, then pressed the button on the cord to answer it.

"Hello?... Hi Jenny... Already?... Well I hope everything's okay... Oh I can do it. No need to track down anyone else... Sure. Can you have Benji handle the Anderson case for me for today? Tell him I'll check in with him later.... Okay. I'm headed to the warehouse then. Mmhmmm. Bye-bye."

She pressed the button on the cord again to hang up, then looked at him. "How would you like to finish delivering backpacks?"

"Backpacks?"

"José did the first round this morning, but his wife thinks she might be in labor. He's gone home, so we'll finish the rest."

He still looked at her, clueless.

"Sheesh, what was in that file other than the fact that I am 30 years old?"

"Well, I know that your favorite color is baby blue, you like Spongebob, you love to read, you're allergic to

60

cats, and you enjoy helping people."

"I'd say that's fairly accurate. Someone did their homework."

The notion puzzled Sebastian. Yes, it did seem that someone had done the necessary research, so how could her age possibly have been overlooked? Either someone had been incredibly careless, or had screwed up big time. He shook his head, mentally setting the thoughts aside. "So tell me about these backpacks…"

"Oh, well… There's an alarming number of children in this city who go hungry over the weekends when they don't have access to school breakfast and lunch. So during the week, Sophie's Wings loads backpacks with enough food to last one child—and sometimes his siblings—through the weekend. We drop the backpacks off at the schools, where the child takes it home in place of his regular backpack, and returns with it on Monday."

"Do you have to go back on Monday to get empty backpacks?"

"No. The schools collect the empty backpacks and make sure all are returned, but we have two sets. So we'll pick up the empties when we drop off the full ones."

"Sounds like a great program. Did you think of it?"

"I wish I could take credit for it, but we're part of a national network of non-profit organizations that have similar programs."

Sebastian nodded, impressed that anyone had thought of such a thing, and even more so that Sophie's Wings helped proliferate it.

When Kelsey pulled the truck to a stop in the 'Director' parking space outside the admin office of a large warehouse, he unbuckled and prepared to get out.

But Kelsey didn't.

She sighed deeply and sat back in her seat after turning the truck off. "I hate coming here unless I absolutely have to—I forget sometimes." She laughed nervously, sadness flickering across her face.

"Why?"

"Bad memories."

She didn't immediately expound, so he merely sat quietly while she tapped her fingers on the steering wheel and stared unseeing at the building.

"My dad died here," she said suddenly. "About four years ago."

This information surprised him. "I'm sorry," he said.

"Yeah, me too. It takes longer to get over the sudden losses, I think. That's probably why my dad never quite got over losing my mom."

"How did he die? An accident?"

Chapter Seven

"Massive heart attack." Kelsey brushed her hair out of her face as she remembered that fateful day. It was a Saturday, so technically the warehouse was closed. But Daddy was there anyway.

She got the call at about 9:00 am.

"Kelsey," her father gasped. *"My chest... I can't breathe!"*

"Daddy! Did you call 911?"

"No. Called you."

"Hang on, I'll be right there! DON'T DIE!"

She'd hung up and quickly called 911 as she dashed around her apartment, locating purse and keys. Then she slammed the phone down and bolted out the door. The paramedics were already here at the warehouse when she arrived. They tried in vain to revive him, all the way into the ambulance and out onto the highway, they pushed on his chest, used the defibrillator, tried to force oxygen into his lungs. She'd followed the ambulance to the hospital, but she knew he was already gone. Dead on arrival, as they put it.

For a long time she had cursed him for calling her, rather than paramedics. He might have survived if he'd gotten medical attention sooner. But then again, maybe not. The doctors said her father had probably been having significant chest pains for weeks, but apparently ignored them.

She shook her head now, clearing her thoughts. "That's why I'm Executive Director instead of my dad. He'd always intended for me to take over for him, just not so soon. He worked himself into the grave, doing his utmost to help others, but at the same time a slave to the memory of my mother."

Sebastian didn't know what to say. He could sense a measure of fear in her, as though she were afraid she might be headed for the same fate, except as a slave to the memory of her father rather than her mother.

She sighed again, then opened the door of the truck. Sebastian did the same as she retrieved a small duffel bag from behind her seat. He gathered up the wrappings and cups from their lunch and followed her into the building.

Twenty minutes later, they had left her truck at the warehouse and were driving a large van, winding down residential streets to the first school on their route.

"Do you always keep jeans and sneakers in your truck?"

"Yep. A whole change of clothes. You never know when things are gonna get grungy. Running deliveries is pretty tame compared to some of the stuff we get into. Particularly after floods or fires or things like that."

"You handle disaster relief, too?"

"Sure. We have bins loaded with blankets, kids clothes diapers, and canned milk, ready to go at a moment's notice. When an entire apartment building burns, the Red Cross is often overloaded and FEMA has larger disasters to worry about. So we step in and help however we can. Sometimes it's just manpower, helping people sort through scorched or soggy belongings to find anything salvageable."

"I thought when you got to be executive director, you didn't have to do that stuff anymore."

She shrugged as she pulled the van to a stop outside

a large elementary school. "I like working with people. I like to see directly the impact Sophie's Wings has on people's lives. When you sit behind a desk all day, I think you kind of get detached from the reality of people's situations."

Sebastian sat somewhat dumbfounded for a few moments after Kelsey got out. Behind a desk…or focusing on individual kids for a couple hundred years. He knew that one kid here and another kid there needed a Faerie Guardian, but he'd completely lost sight of the big picture—of the reality of people's situations.

He heard the back door of the van being rolled up, and quickly got out and went around to help Kelsey.

They loaded three bins, each holding six backpacks, onto a flatbed handcart. Kelsey grabbed two more bags and set them on top.

"This many at one school?"

"Yeah, but this is a large school. Some schools have only five or six who need them. I think we average eight to ten per school.

"And how many schools?"

"Sixteen."

"That's a lot of kids."

Kelsey nodded. "We do what we can."

Sebastian took the handle of the handcart and pushed it toward the building. "So I guess Sophie's is a sort of Faerie Guardian to all those kids, with you as head Godmother, huh?"

She gave him a reproving smile. "The politically correct term is the genderless 'Executive Director' these days."

"Ah," he nodded with a grin. "Of course."

They discreetly unloaded the bins containing full backpacks outside the front office, then retrieved three bins stacked together with all the empties piled into the top bin.

"That was rather anti-climactic," Sebastian said on the way back to the van.

"How so?"

"I guess I was expecting to see the kids, see the appreciation in their eyes."

Kelsey shook her head. "We rarely ever see the kids. Most are embarrassed that they need our help, and a few are even resentful." She shrugged a shoulder, as though it were neither here nor there. "But that doesn't change the fact that they need to eat."

"Don't you ever get any thanks?"

"Oh, certainly. We have the gratitude of the staff of the schools, who might otherwise have to watch these kids slowly starve. And we do occasionally get a drawing or letter returned in an empty, from a child or a mom. But the real thanks is in knowing we're doing something worthwhile. That these kids are getting enough to eat even when the school can't personally feed them."

They visited seven more schools in similar fashion, then headed back to the warehouse, where they unloaded the empty bins. Then they unstacked all of them, including the ones José had picked up earlier, and placed six empty backpacks in each, unzipping them and making them ready to be filled again.

Somewhere in the middle, Sebastian found a folded piece of paper in the bottom of one empty backpack. He stood and carefully opened it to see a picture of three stick kids, one of whom carried a red backpack. The other two each had small round red and orange objects in their hands that might be apples and oranges. Off to the side was a carefully drawn swing set and slide.

Dear Sofys wings,
  Tank you verry much for the rice and froot.
I don like the tuna but my mom makes me eet it.

66

Fairy Godlover

She says it good for me. I like chikin best. Tank you.

Love Joshua B.

A warm fuzzy feeling seeped through him and he took the letter to Kelsey.

"See? I told you this job wasn't totally thankless." She grinned and pointed him to a bulletin board where several other such letters were tacked.

He proudly pinned Joshua's alongside the others.

* * *

Sebastian gazed at Kelsey as she slept, wondering at the stroke of providence that got him assigned as her guardian. She was a remarkable woman, and his heart grew tight at the thought that his time with her was limited.

He wanted to wake her up and make love to her again, to cram as much time together as he could into whatever time he had left. But he knew she was exhausted. She had run non-stop all day. Except for the short interlude in the elevator, she hadn't taken any time for herself. When they'd returned home from Sophie's, she'd changed her clothes—into a long t-shirt and sweatshorts—while he microwaved some dinners for them. After they ate, she had settled with him on the couch to watch the local and national news.

He'd looked down at her mid-way through the national news to find that she was fast asleep.

So he'd watched the rest of the news, and the odd assortment of sitcoms and dramas that had come on after. Well... he didn't really watch them. He watched Kelsey more than the television. He'd savored the feel of her in his arms, of her nuzzling sleepily against his chest. He'd enjoyed her contented sighs and dreamy murmurs. The way her unbound nipples poked through her t-shirt in response to whatever she was dreaming. Then when the local news had come on again, he'd carried her to her bed, removed her shorts with a silent Guardian command, and tucked her in.

* * *

Kelsey emerged from her bedroom the following morning—she couldn't believe she'd fallen dead asleep like that—to find Sebastian in the kitchen wearing only a pair of navy blue boxer shorts and looking more than a little befuddled.

Her heart leapt at the sight of his bare chest and tousled hair. "Sebastian? What's the matter?"

"I was trying to make you some coffee without magic, but I have no idea how to work this thing." He held up the pitcher from her blender. "Where do you put the coffee grounds?"

She tried unsuccessfully not to smile. "Kids aren't big coffee drinkers, I guess. I appreciate the effort, though." She snorted a little with the effort of holding back a laugh.

"Oh-kay…Go ahead. I can see you're trying not to laugh. What did I do?"

"Well… that's not the coffee maker. It's a blender."

He looked at the piece in his hand, and Kelsey was shocked to see a bit of color stain his cheeks. "Ah. That explains a lot," he said, somewhat sheepishly.

Still grinning, Kelsey opened a cupboard and brought down the coffee maker, which she only used on the weekends—weekdays she drove through Java Joe's for her cheap morning jolt—another of the few luxuries she squeezed into her budget.

She showed him how to scoop coffee into a filter and pour water into the reservoir as he watched intently. Soon fresh-brewed coffee was dribbling into the pot, filling the small kitchen with its aroma.

"That was easy," he said when the brewing was well underway.

"When you use the right machine." She opened the

refrigerator and got a breakfast bar from a box on the door. "Help yourself to whatever I have. It's probably slim pickin's though. There are breakfast bars here, probably some cereal in that cupboard, and maybe some waffles in the freezer."

"Is that all you're having?" He motioned to the bar in her hand.

"Yep. Lots of vitamins, minerals, and a good bit of protein, too." She opened the wrapper and made her way into the dining room to sit down.

"And carbs for energy?"

Kelsey nodded and took a bite while Sebastian poured two mugs of coffee. He carried both to the table and set one in front of her.

"So what's on the agenda for today?" he asked as he sat down, leaning forward to rest his arms on the table.

Kelsey inhaled the steam from her mug and smiled blissfully. "Just a couple of loads of laundry. And some grocery shopping. Maybe sweep and mop, clean the bathrooms, stuff like that."

"That's all? No meetings? No deliveries?"

"That's all. Why?"

"Just curious…" He leaned back in his chair and shrugged innocently, but she didn't miss the sly smile tugging at the corner of his mouth—or the tent in his shorts.

She pretended not to notice—even though her body reacted swiftly to the sight, becoming wet almost instantly—as she chewed and swallowed another bite of bar. "Is there someplace you wanted to go?" she asked, an equal measure of innocence in her voice.

"Definitely, but it's not far away." He slid out of his chair to crouch on the floor.

"Oh?" Her wanton body tingled deliciously as she finished her breakfast bar. "Did you need to buy something?"

He shook his head. "Where I want to go isn't a store. It's someplace to *eat*."

"Mmm…I see. Do you need me to go with you?"

He moved to kneel between her knees and slid his hands up her bare legs. "I definitely need you to come." He grasped her hips and pulled her to the edge of the chair. Then he lifted her shirt and began to nuzzle her breasts, the ridge of his erection caressing her sex.

What a way to start a morning!

"Would you like to come, Kelsey?"

She nodded, her body already trembling with anticipation.

He drew one nipple into her mouth and tugged it gently with his teeth before releasing it and giving it a sensuous lick. "Tell me." He did the same to the other nipple.

"I—I want to come," she whispered, her cheeks heating as she said the words.

His finger slid under the front of her thong, then slowly traced the edge of it down over her pubic hair, until his knuckle brushed her already wet clit. He stroked the knuckle through her slick fold and chuckled. "That didn't take long. Your body flatters me…"

She could only nod since his stroking made it difficult to concentrate on voluntary responses.

His voice grew dark. "Soft and slow or hard and fast?"

"Wha—?"

"How do you want to come, Kelsey?"

Uhnh! Too many choices! "Hard… and fast."

Before the words were completely out of her mouth, he plunged two long fingers into her sheath, curling them to press against the front wall of her vagina as he thrust in and out.

"Oh! Ohhhhhhh…" She slid down further, spread her legs wide, giving him better access.

His mouth kissed down her stomach, over her pubic mound, to her pussy, where he nuzzled and tugged at her labia with his lips.

"Pinch your nipples, Kelsey, tug them hard…"

Without a word she obeyed, squeezing her nipples between her fingers, pulling the tender flesh as his mouth suckled and pulled on her nether-lips.

He looked up at her as he drew her inner lips into his mouth. Their eyes met as he suckled, and—she felt a fluttering pressure over her anus.

She gasped and her eyes closed as she concentrated on the sensation. It was his finger. While one hand continued to plunge in and out of her cunt, his other hand massaging her from front to back. She couldn't help but moan louder whenever his finger touched that sensitive entrance. With every pass it lingered longer and longer, drawing louder and louder moans from her.

His mouth now concentrated on her clit, suckling and nibbling, and the fingers in her sheath now moved in small circles over a particularly sensitive spot on her vaginal wall. Tension built in her pelvis and began sparking out to the rest of her body, building, building…

She sank the fingers of one hand into his hair, her hips bucking against his mouth, moaning uncontrollably as she teetered on the brink.

The finger at her anus pressed inside—just slightly—and she burst. Wave upon wave of electric pleasure crashed through her body, jolting every nerve ending. Her voice echoed off the dining room walls, a long fervent wail.

She gradually returned to her senses and realized she was squeezing his head between her thighs. Embarrassed and still twitching, she opened her legs. "Sorry," she said meekly, but couldn't prevent a grin.

"I think I'll recover." He returned the grin, then gave her one final lick, which made her gasp, before righting her panties and shirt. "Shall we do laundry now?"

"Wha—What about you?" She sat up in the chair as he stood.

"I've got all day, and I intend to use it…"

"Now wait a minute. That hardly seems fair, especially given your resilience." She snagged the waistband of his shorts with a trembling hand to prevent him from walking away. The action pulled the fabric away from his skin and allowed his raging erection to spring upright. The head of his cock winked invitingly at her, and she licked her lips. "You get to tease my body to orgasm, but I don't get to do the same to yours?" She lifted her gaze to meet his.

He was surprised, she could tell, but he rolled with it, a sexy smile on those seductive lips. "Well, when you put it that way, I guess it doesn't seem fair."

"That's what I thought." She grinned and lifted her other hand to tug his shorts further down, until they dipped below his scrotum and slid down his hips. "It's been a while since I've done this, but I imagine it's like riding a bike." Now she wrapped one hand around his girth—her thumb and fingers *almost* met—and cupped his balls with the other as she dragged her tongue up the underside of his shaft.

He hissed in a breath, then let it out slowly. "How long?" A bit of concern tinged his voice.

"Since college." Her tongue darted out to capture the bead of pre-cum that had appeared at his tip, and she grinned when his dick twitched in response. "Guys like teeth, right? Love bites?" She took him into her mouth before she could laugh or before he could do anything more than give a panicked grunt.

Her lips stretched around him and she slid her head down as far as she could, until his tip touched the back of her throat. Luckily the skill she'd practiced with cucumbers so many years ago hadn't left her, and she didn't gag as she held him there for long moments, swirling her tongue around him and massaging the lower half of his shaft with her hand.

He groaned his surprised appreciation. "Oh god baby, that feels so good."

His praise urged her on, making her pussy begin to tingle with renewed desire as she began to milk his cock with her mouth, moving her head back to create suction with her cheeks and sliding her hand down, then moving her mouth down again while sliding her hand up to meet her lips.

She'd never actually enjoyed doing this for a man when she was younger. She'd done it for the sole purpose of pleasing her lovers—usually when she wasn't in the mood for awkward groping or tentative sex.

But taking Sebastian into her mouth now and pleasuring him this way was an entirely different experience. She was truly enjoying this, enjoying the taste of him, the texture and firmness of him. And the longer she worked, the more voracious she became, eagerly licking and sucking, not only because he so obviously enjoyed it, but because it made *her* incredibly hot, too.

His hips began to move in time with her mouth, meeting her half-way and thrusting himself further down her throat, murmuring searing encouragement between gasps and groans.

She felt his fingers trailing softly through her hair, and she looked up at him, meeting his glassy gold gaze. "God I love your lips wrapped around me," he said, his voice low and gravelly.

She smiled and released him with a slight popping sound as the suction broke, then ducked her head to lick his balls, taking first one, then the other into her mouth, suckling gently. When she returned to his cock, he seemed larger, harder, and more urgent. Their pace increased and her impassioned cries matched his, until she felt his balls suddenly tighten in her hand.

"Kelsey—" His fingers tightened in her hair.

"Mmmmm…"

His hips twitched and bucked. "Oh god, Kelsey—I can't hold back—"

She sucked harder, stroked harder with her hand.

"Keeellllseeey!" he roared as he jetted hot sperm down her throat, slamming himself into her mouth. She swallowed quickly but couldn't keep up with the copious flow, and she felt some of the hot liquid dribble down her chin. When his cock went limp, she gave one last suck and slowly drew back, sitting primly in her chair.

"Now we can do laundry if you'd like." She smiled sweetly up at him and licked the dribble of come from her chin.

He sank back into the wooden chair, still breathing hard, his spent cock flopping across his thigh. Then he laughed, a deep sexy sound that curled her toes. "You are an amazing woman, Kelsey Schroder."

"And don't you forget it," she said saucily, then got up to take their dishes to the dishwasher. She felt his gaze on her ass, so she swayed her hips back and forth in an exaggerated sashay. On her way back through, she planted a lusty kiss on his lips, making sure he could taste himself in her mouth. Then she continued down the hall to gather her laundry.

After a few moments, he tucked himself back into his shorts and got up to follow her.

Chapter Eight

A while later, they lay on the couch as Kelsey told Sebastian more about Sophie's Wings and how she came to be Executive Director, aside from being the daughter of the founder.

Sebastian had lay down to 'recover' from Kelsey's talented ministrations. She had sat down in the chair, but had gradually moved to the other end of the couch, and eventually stretched out alongside him.

"I volunteered at Wings all through middle school, junior high and high school, working in the warehouse, making copies, that sort of thing."

"Did you enjoy it, or did you do it because your dad wanted you to do it?"

"Both. I liked helping others, and I liked making my dad proud, too."

"I can believe that."

"When I started college, I had to cut way back on my hours at Wings, but that's about the time José showed up, so it worked out."

"Or else you might not have gone?"

"Oh, I would have gone. I hate to admit it, but college was way more important to me than Wings."

"That's really not a bad thing."

"My original plan was to become a CPA and do Wings' tax stuff for free, so that my dad wouldn't have to pay someone to do it every year."

"What happened?"

"Well, I graduated college when I was twenty-three, got licensed and certified almost immediately, and went to work for Huber and Green downtown during the day, while I worked on my Masters at night. Between volunteering at Wings and work, it took me two years to earn my Masters degree. I was making plans to go into business for myself when my dad died."

"And so you took the helm with the blessing of the rest of the Board."

"Yeah. That about sums it up."

"What were you like in college?"

Kelsey shrugged. "I was a big nerd. Honor Society and all that. My grades came first, everything else second. I relied on scholarships, so I couldn't afford to bomb."

"Did you date much?"

"Some. Usually nerdy guys. The cool guys didn't come anywhere near me."

"I find that hard to believe."

"Thanks, I think, but believe it. I might not have dated at all except that I was jealous of all the action Gina got."

"Gina?"

"My best friend and roommate."

"Did you look anything like you do now?"

"My hair was a bit longer, and I wore jeans and t-shirts almost exclusively, but yeah."

"Did you go to a school for the blind?"

Kelsey laughed. "I have a box of pictures in my closet. I can go get it if you want."

He grinned. "Yeah, I love pictures."

She hopped up from the couch and dashed to her bedroom. In the closet, she spied the box of pictures—under her blue box of toys. She reached up and tried to pull the photo box out, but the blue box seemed to be caught on the lid. Bugger. She tried to push both boxes back, but something had apparently fallen behind when she moved them, and now whatever it was prevented the box from sliding back. And if she let go, both would fall. She considered lifting both down, but she didn't think she could hold the weight of both with her arms stretched above her head like this. Which meant she just needed to get up a little higher.

And she needed to hurry before Sebastian came and offered to help. Hmmm... Her eyes fell on the stool and she brought it over with her foot. There, that's better. She stepped up onto the stool but it wasn't over far enough. Drat!

Sebastian appeared in the doorway and saw her precarious perch. "Here, let me help you with that—"

"No, I've got it."

"I can hold the top—"

"It's okay, I've got—" But she didn't. As she watched in horror, both boxes slipped out of her grasp. As though in slow motion, they fell to the carpet. The photo box landed safely between two winter boots and remained intact. But of course the very box she'd been trying so hard to keep him from seeing did not. It bounced slightly, ejected the lid, and spewed its contents over the floor of the closet.

They both stood motionless, looking at the mess.

"An interesting toy collection."

Kelsey groaned as her cheeks flamed. With luck, she would blush so fiercely that she would spontaneously combust and disappear in a poof of smoke.

Sebastian crouched to get a better look, retrieving a huge hot-pink dildo, which protruded obscenely from a conservatively sensible mid-heeled pump. He turned it in his hands, inspecting it without the slightest hint of distaste.

Kelsey waited, but combustion was not forthcoming. Dammit. Well then, what else could she do? "I um…" she began, but no thought attached itself to the statement, so she stood on the step-stool helplessly mute, her face no doubt as pink as that dildo, watching in resigned humiliation.

Sebastian continued to gather the contents of the box: dildos and vibrators of varying shapes, colors, sizes, and uses, as well as lubricant, cleaner, batteries, and a few other naughty toys. His curiosity was evident as he carefully examined each toy, read each label, before placing everything back in the box, a wicked smile tugging at the corners of his mouth. The last thing he picked up was the erotic novel, *Carnal Passions*, featuring two nude bodies entwined on the front cover. He opened the paperback to one of the bookmarks and began to skim pages.

"Sebastian—"

"Hmm?"

"I wish—"

He looked up, eyes smoldering, that wicked smile still on his lips. "What do you wish?"

"I—" She had started to say 'I wish you wouldn't read that,' but she couldn't utter it, because it wasn't true. What she really wanted was to experience untamed, uninhibited, uncontrolled naked lust with him. For most of her adult life she'd yearned to explore, to experiment, to discover what lay in that steamy, darkly tempting world of carnal passion. But her conservative upbringing and lack of time unfortunately hampered anything but solo discovery.

"What do you want, Kelsey? Tell me."

Her eyes were drawn to his shorts, where his cock strained valiantly at the thin material. She returned her gaze to his. "I—I want to play."

"How do you want to play?"

"I want—" She hesitated, unsure whether she had

the nerve to articulate what she wanted. But his eyes burned into hers, seeming to say *Tell me, please.* "I want to umm…" Her heart thundered in her chest, making her breathless. "I want to be fucked in ways I've never been fucked before," she blurted, blushing as she said it. When it was out, she pressed her lips together, as though doing so might prevent further outburst.

The wicked smile was replaced by dark, heated lust. His eyes nearly ignited. "Anything particular in mind?"

"Anything."

His cock twitched in his shorts. "Anything?"

She could only nod, her head spinning a bit. Her heart was pounding so hard now she was sure he could hear it.

He closed the book and placed it in the top of the box, then held out his hand to her. A silent invitation.

Without hesitation, she put her hand in his, felt his hot skin against hers, felt the pulse in his fingertips. A thrill of anticipation shot straight to her core.

Wordlessly, he led her out of the closet and brought her to a stop beside the bed. Without either of them moving, the curtains closed, and the lights switched off, leaving them standing in the dim glow of daylight through the window coverings.

He held the box out to her. "Choose one," he commanded, his voice gravelly and hoarse.

With much less embarrassment than she would have expected she considered the contents of the box, and after a few moments, chose a slim, green, vaguely penis-shaped, jelly dildo with a wide base.

After selecting a tube of lubricant, he placed the box on the bedside table. Then he took the green dong from her and tossed it on the bed with the lubricant.

Then, unexpectedly, he folded her into his arms, his rock-hard erection pressing into her stomach. His muscles were tight, his body rigid, restrained. The noise of their combined heartbeats was nearly deafening, and she realized he was nearly as crazy with lust as she. Perhaps they both needed a moment to reign in their feral passions before somebody got hurt—probably her.

He took a deep breath and she did the same, unconsciously synchronizing her body to his. She hardly noticed that her pulse had slowed or that her mind had cleared—until his hands moved down her body and grasped the hem of her t-shirt.

She raised her hands as he peeled the material up over her head and tossed it aside. Then she settled her hands on his hips and raised her lips for a kiss.

He obliged, his hands skimming the skin of her back, and grasping the string waistband, he tugged her thong upwards, making the material scrape against her anus. She sighed against his lips and he did it again.

"If I'm to accommodate you," he said as his mouth left hers to nibble down her neck, "I need to know how you *have* been fucked before." He bit the tender area where her neck and shoulder met, then soothed the spot with his tongue.

She groaned as he nibbled another spot on her shoulder and his fingers found her aching clit through the lace of her panties. "By another person?"

He chuckled against her. "Yes, by another person. Self pleasure is nice but not quite the same."

She freed his cock from his shorts and pushed the fabric over his hips until it fell to the floor. Then she took him in her hands and stroked gently. In response, his teeth sank into her shoulder and he roughly pulled her thong down her legs until it too slid to the floor.

"Standard missionary," she gasped as he pinched her clit between two fingers, then stroked soothingly over it. "Umm…" *What was she saying?* "Limited oral."

His head came up, leaving her feeling a bit bereft. Fortunately his fingers continued stroking. "That's it?"

"Until you." Her head bobbed impatiently and she pulled his head back to her neck. "I don't have time to cultivate—" the fingers of his other hand slid between the cheeks of her ass and stroked lightly over the puckered opening as his teeth once again nibbled her neck, "—the sort of trusting...relationship—" she fought hard to hang on to the train of thought, "—required for more decadent...exploits."

He lifted his head again, but his fingers continued to torment her. "Do you trust *me*?"

She could only nod.

"Hang on," he said, and listed backward without warning, pulling her with him.

"Oh!" She braced herself against him as first he bounced prone on the bed, then she bounced, laughing, on top of him. "What was that?"

"I like it when women fall all over me."

"Ohhh," she groaned, and swatted his arm. When they stopped bouncing, he treated her to a devilish smile. Then she realized the placement of his hands, and more specifically, his fingers. Splayed over her ass, his fingers dipped into the crease, his forefingers teasing her labia, and his middle fingers tantalizingly close to her anus. "Ohhh," she groaned again, this time with anticipation. She loved stimulation there, and often fantasized about being taken that way. Maybe...?

His eyes grew dark, his expression heated, as though he were reading her thoughts. It was entirely possible, she realized, but at this moment she didn't care. His fingers pressed a little harder, his hands squeezed, pressing her hips against his cock trapped between them. Then his hands retreated and he rolled with her, pulling her beneath him.

"Anything, Kelsey?" he asked, voice tight.

She met his gaze, her own eyes burning. "Anything."

He reached for something beside her on the bed, held it up. The green dildo.

"Have you ever used this thing to fuck yourself in the ass?"

Her cheeks flamed. "Yes," she admitted softly.

His eyes burned into her, his jaw set, as he sat back. "Turn over."

She quickly obeyed, and as she did so, a large pillow appeared under her hips, tilting her ass into the air, her head and shoulders resting on the rumpled sheets.

She gasped as his teeth bit into the flesh of her ass, as his hands squeezed and pulled. The sensation was so erotic it nearly sent her over the edge right then, but she took a deep breath and concentrated on his mouth. "Oohh, yeah."

His tongue speared into her cunt and licked her inner walls, then moved up, over her perineum, to circle her anus. She cried out, her legs trembling.

"Has any man ever touched you here, Kelsey?" He pressed his tongue against her to illustrate.

She shook her head. "Only you," she managed in a small squeak.

"But you like it, *don't you*?"

She nodded.

"Tellll me, Kellllsey." On each 'L' sound he licked her again. Her cunt wept at the sensation; she knew she must be dripping by now.

"Yes! Ohhhoohh, I like it," she sobbed, hands fisting in the sheets. "I like it!"

He opened the tube of lubricant and liberally drizzled it over her. Then he coated the dildo and slid it lengthwise between her ass cheeks. "What do you want me to do with this slippery little bugger?"

"Unhhh…" she said, biting the mattress. Could she say it? Would he make her?

She didn't have to wait to find out. Mercifully, he didn't linger for her to answer further, and instead pressed the tip of the dildo against her anus. Breathless, she bore down a bit and let out a long sighing moan as he slid it slowly inside.

Sebastian nearly lost it right there on the sheets, watching that green jelly disappear into her ass, seeing the involuntary bucking of her hips, the writhing of her body as he pumped the dildo in and out, hearing her escalating cries of passion. *Get a grip, Sebastian.* His cock jerked at the thought and he smiled. Then he dipped his head to suckle her clit, but the moment he touched his tongue to her, she screamed his name, coming violently.

All thought toward restraint fled with the quaking of her body, urgent need ricocheted through him, and the only thing Sebastian could focus on was getting inside her. He scrambled to his knees behind her, and leaving the dildo where it was, he plunged into her wet sheath.

That unnerving fuzzy sensation washed over him as he began to pound into her, and she groaned as she no doubt felt it, too. What the hell was that, and why did it feel so damned good?

Kelsey raised herself up on her hands and knees, panting anew. She ground her pelvis against him, causing the silicone of the dildo to pull at the skin of his abdomen but he hardly noticed. His fingers dug into the flesh of her hips as he clung desperately, fighting for control. If he lost it now, he'd leave her hanging.

He looked down and saw that each time he withdrew, so did the dildo—just a bit. And each time he slammed into her, he shoved the dildo back into her ass. *Ohhhhh,* he groaned, nearly mindless.

She was keening now, on the brink of another orgasm, and he could no longer hold back. With a primal roar, he spilled himself into her, spurting again and again, so powerfully he though he might never stop coming.

Moments later, she shrieked as another violent orgasm gripped her. His hips still pumping, he sat back on his heels, pulling her with him and holding her body against his until the tremors gripping her body eased in intensity. Then he slowly stilled his hips.

They sat like that for long moments, struggling to fill their lungs. Gradually he became aware that he held her nipples between his fingers, and he let go to gently cup her breasts.

"Sebastian." She whispered, awe in her voice.

"Kelsey," he said, equally inspired.

Then the only sound was their ragged breathing, which gradually slowed as he stroked her breasts and belly.

After a while, she shifted uncomfortably. "I think I need to get this thing out of my ass."

He grinned and bent her forward, carefully so as not to disengage himself. "No problem," he said, and gently withdrew the dildo. Her anus gaped open for a few seconds before relaxing into pucker mode again.

The sight caused his cock to stir inside her and he brought her upright again, tossed the dildo aside. His hands returned to cup her breast, and he settled his mouth on her neck. This felt nice. Buried to the hilt in Kelsey, her breasts almost filling his hands, her sated body limp against him. He could get used to this.

No he couldn't, he reminded himself. He would surely be reassigned any day now. He would have to leave Kelsey and all these warm fuzzy feelings behind and return to his normal duties.

Don't think about that now. Enjoy the moment, enjoy the woman.

"That almost scared the hell out of me," she confessed, her voice somewhat hoarse, bringing his thoughts back to the moment. "I've never ever felt anything so powerful. I wasn't sure I could survive it."

"Mmm… It was pretty powerful," he agreed. "I thought I'd never stop spurting. I never knew I could produce such volume."

Kelsey chuckled, which caused said volume to seep out where they remained joined.

"I should probably get in the shower before I squish too much more," she said.

"I'll wash up the little green man and strip the sheets."

She agreed and lifted herself off of him, pecked a kiss on his cheek, then quickly dashed to the bathroom.

He flopped onto the bed wondering if *he'd* survive many more orgasms like that.

Chapter Nine

"Can I still look at the pictures?"

She grinned and pushed her plate away. "Sure. They're in my closet."

"The box that landed without incident?"

"That would be the one."

"Be right back." He sprinted down the hallway and she leaned out to watch his ass as he went. They had prepared and eaten lunch in the nude, a new experience for Kelsey. She didn't realize she liked being naked so much—and in the middle of the day!—until there were appreciative eyes to enjoy her nudity. And maybe it was her imagination, but the ramen noodles with broccoli and chunk chicken had somehow tasted better than usual.

Sebastian returned, his semi-erect cock swaying as he walked, and set the box between them with a smirk. "Were you checking me out?"

"Absolutely."

He winked at her. "Okay, just making sure." Sitting once more, he gestured to the box. "Would you like to do the honors?"

"You go ahead. There's nothing in *that* box worth hiding."

"Nothing worth hiding in the other box, either." He flipped the lid open and scooped out a handful of photographs.

"A large segment of the population would disagree

with you."

"That's their problem." He held up the first picture
on the stack, a yellowed photograph of a young couple
standing in front of a white clapboard house, squinting
into the sun. "Who's this?"

"That's my mom and dad. My mom was pregnant
with me then—see?" She indicated the woman's gently
swollen belly.

He looked at the picture again. "You look a lot like
her."

"I know. My dad always told me that." And always
with a tinge of sadness. She sighed and sorted through
more photos until she found one of a young dark-haired
woman in a skin-tight black jumpsuit. "And here's Gina.
She hasn't changed much either. Still dresses like that at
every opportunity."

"Who's this guy?" Sebastian held up a photo of a
younger Kelsey sitting on the lap of a good-looking blond
man.

"Oh, that's Brian, better known as 'Shithead' in conversation these days."

"You have quite a few pictures of you and him together."

"That's because I was young and naïve and flattered
that he had noticed me. I thought he was so cute, and
loved to have my picture taken with him."

"What happened?"

"I finally figured out he had all the personality of a
deflated balloon."

"Brian, or his dick?"

"Yes." She rolled her eyes and shook her head.

"He couldn't get it up? He looks so young!"

"He was twenty-four. He went out with me to prove
to himself he wasn't gay, but I ended up proving just the
opposite. How's *that* for a compliment?"

Sebastian couldn't help but laugh. "I can see how that might be a little tough on the ego." It was clear that Kelsey carried no flame for Brian, but he sensed the experience had perhaps bruised her self-esteem. "I'm pretty sure his sexual preferences were not a result of anything you did."

"I know. But that's kinda when I decided I wasn't going to settle for good looks and mediocrity." She tilted her head and looked at the picture in her hand. "The man I eventually settle down with definitely cannot be—or have—a deflated balloon."

"A valid standard if I ever heard one." He leaned back in his chair, tilting his hips so his cock jutted into the air. "Speaking of which, I have a very *un*-deflated balloon that could be put to some use."

"Ooh! Balloon animals!" she cried jubilantly, feasting her eyes on his long shaft.

He visibly cringed and she laughed, and kept laughing as she straddled his chair and proceeded to joyfully impale herself on him repeatedly.

* * *

Kelsey shoved her front door open and struggled to extricate the key from the lock while Sebastian carried in an armload of groceries behind her. "I could swear we didn't put this many bags *in* the truck." The key finally came loose and she dropped the whole key ring on the dining room table on her way into the kitchen to set her bag on the counter. "Did they manage to multiply on the way home?"

Sebastian shrugged innocently and headed back outside to get the last of the bags. When he returned, he kicked the door closed behind him and joined her in the kitchen. Together they unloaded the bags.

"Okay, now I'm sure I didn't buy this." Kelsey held up a bottle of chocolate syrup.

"So the bags *did* multiply on the way home," he said with exaggerated amazement. Then he winked and held up a jar of maraschino cherries. "Where do you want me to put these?"

"Cherries? I didn't buy cherries."

"Oh, well then I'll just take care of these."

"Where are you going?" She asked this to his back as he headed down the hall and into her bedroom.

"To put them away," he called.

She heard a drawer open and close. "In my dresser?"

A few moments later he rejoined her in the kitchen, his eyes glittering with mischief. "Bedside table. You never know when you're going to need a midnight snack."

"I see."

"I think maybe you do." Sebastian returned to rummaging around in bags, looking for the box of cookies he knew he'd put in there somewhere.

But another small box at the bottom of one of the bags caught his attention. Magnum Extra Large? He grinned and held up a box of condoms. "If *I* didn't put this in here—" The ringing of Kelsey's mobile phone cut him short.

Her cheeks pink, she scrambled for her purse amid the grocery bags, found her phone, and flipped it open. "Hello?… Hi José… Ohhhh, that's wonderful! Congratulations!… Reina Catharina, that's beautiful… Oh, thanks for calling, sweetie. I'm so glad everyone's doing well… Okay, give Dia a big hug for me, and I insist you take the week off… Yes, do not come into work, we can manage for a week… You too… Bye-bye." She flipped the phone closed and turned to him, beaming. "José is a daddy! They had a healthy baby girl early this morning."

Sebastian's heart flip-flopped in his chest and his breath stalled in his lungs. Crazy thoughts flitted through his head, all of them having to do with Kelsey and babies with dark hair and misty gray eyes.

Cut it out, he scolded himself. Temporary assignment, pleasant diversion, itch-scratching and all that.

Yeah.

Sure.

"You okay?"

He blinked and focused his gaze on her face as she looked at him, concern evident in her eyes. Offering her a smile, he shrugged. "Just thinking that José must have had a rough night."

Her smile returned. "Not as rough as Dia."

"True."

"Can I make a wish?"

"Absolutely. Have at it."

"I wish for three packages of diapers, and I wish them to be in the back seat of Jose's car."

"Done."

* * *

After all the groceries had been put away and Kelsey had quickly stashed the box of condoms out of sight, she stripped naked again and removed the French braid from her still-damp hair. She had showered quickly before heading out to the grocery store, and had almost resented having to put clothes on to go. Who knew she was a closet nudist, too?

She shook out her hair and finger-combed it as she returned to the living room.

Sebastian's eyebrows rose when he saw her.

"I think I like being naked."

He pulled her into his lap. "I definitely like you being naked."

"I can tell." The evidence pressed against her thigh. Feeling suddenly frisky and bold, she leaned in to kiss him, sweeping her tongue into his mouth to tangle with his. He groaned and pulled her closer, adjusting her so that she straddled him. Eagerly she wrapped her arms around his neck, buried her hands in his dark hair, her nipples grazing the fabric of his shirt.

He sucked her tongue gently, creating similar sensations between her legs, heightened by his hands gripping her ass and moving her against him.

Remarkably, she felt herself ascending toward ecstasy after only a few breathless minutes. She wantonly pressed her breasts against his chest, ground her hips against his, rubbing her clit against his jeans. *So close... so close!*

She gasped into his mouth as the orgasm crashed over her. Through her haze, she felt him smile, then pull back and touch his forehead to hers.

"Why don't you wish something for *you*?" he asked when she had recovered slightly. "Something you've always wanted but never got."

What? Her passion-fogged brain reeled. Didn't he want to fuck her brains out after that? *Please?!* "I already did."

"When?"

"I wished for wild wanton sex."

"First of all, you didn't technically wish it. You said 'I want', not 'I wish.' And second of all, two kinds of requests don't count as wishes: Things that are already done, in progress or going to happen anyway, and things that are a pleasure to do and don't require much magic."

"Really?"

"Absolutely. So think of something else. Something that *will* require magic."

"Okay…" Her head cleared slightly, and she thought of one thing she'd wanted since she was in high school. "I wish... I wish I had larger breasts."

"Declined."

She blinked. "Pardon?"

"Declined." He bent his head to nuzzle one of the

91

breasts in question. "They're perfect the way they are."

"But—"

"No buts. Wish for something else."

She crossed her arms over her chest, cutting off his access. "No."

"Tell me more about that box."

Huh? The question caught Kelsey completely off guard and she blushed. "Ummm?"

"And don't you dare say 'what box.' You know which box I'm talking about." He smiled knowingly, somehow anticipating her thoughts. Then he dipped his head and triumphantly took a nipple into his mouth.

"Ohh!" She hadn't realized she'd dropped her arms again. Heat spiraled through her again.

He straightened and looked at her expectantly.

"What do you want to know?" she asked carefully.

"Did *you* buy them?"

"Most of them. Gina gave me one or two."

"You and she are still good friends?"

Kelsey nodded. "She calls me a closet nympho."

He grinned. "That's cute."

"She thinks so, too."

"Have you used all of them?"

"Of course."

"Is the green one your favorite?"

"No."

His eyes widened with surprise. "No?"

She shook her head.

"Then why did you choose it earlier?"

"It was the least obscene."

"Which one's your favorite?"

She was quiet for a few moments, because truthfully she had several favorites, depending on her mood. But if she had to choose just one... "The pink one," she finally said, meekly.

"That great big one?"

She nodded, knowing her cheeks must be as bright as the dildo they were discussing.

He grinned like a Cheshire cat. "Well that explains it."

"Explains what?"

"Why you weren't too tight to take me after four years without sex. That thing must have kept you pretty stretched."

Kelsey thought she detected a trace of jealousy in his voice, but she couldn't be sure. She looked up at him but he only smiled. She decided to let it go, and put a different spin on it. "Is that a twinge of *cock*iness I hear in your voice?"

"Damn straight. Most of us get to choose our bodies when we first start out, so male Guardians tend to be on the larger side."

"Well, I'm glad I had 'that thing.' It would have been a bummer to have a six foot specimen of well-hung man appear out of thin air in my bedroom and be too small to do anything with him, now wouldn't it?"

He stroked a finger between the cheeks of her ass. "Have you used that thing to—"

"No," she said quickly, then added with a coy smile, "Not yet anyway."

He raised an eyebrow but thankfully didn't comment. "Tell me more about your sexual interests."

"Really?"

"Really."

"What if you think they're too weird?"

"I fucked you in an elevator and with a dildo in your ass. You really think I'm gonna think something's too weird?"

No, she guessed not. She shrugged. "My interest is in sex. Period. In my head, there are very few things I'd

93

say no to without trying them—so long as all participants are healthy consenting adults and remain so. But my actual experience is fairly limited." She grinned. "I should have been a porn star."

"What do you fantasize about?"

"The real thing. Vibrators are great, but not nearly as good as actual flesh—most of the time."

"Okay, how about this? If you were a sex goddess for a day, what would you do?"

"For a day? Hmmm… I would… wear a black leather corset… with spiked heels."

"Panties?"

"Nah. I'd want easy access."

"How would you take your pleasure?"

"By fulfilling my lover's fantasy."

"What if you found your lover's fantasy objectionable?"

She thought for a moment. "I'd probably try it anyway, because I might find I like it. Besides, I would find pleasure in my lover's pleasure."

"Honestly?"

She nodded. "But that's only if I could be a sex goddess for a *day*. If I had more than one day, I'm sure I could find some fantasy of my own to act out."

"I don't doubt it."

Her stomach rumbled softly, but she ignored it, instead concentrating on the feeling of his erection between her legs, which seemed to have swelled even more during their conversation.

"Are you hungry?" he asked.

"Is that a trick question?"

"Not intentionally."

She backed off his lap and knelt on the floor before him. "I've made two discoveries today." Her hands worked at his belt as he watched. She chuckled softly at the wet spot she'd created on the front of his jeans.

"Have you?"

She eased his zipper down and freed him from the waistband of his boxers. "The second one I already told you—I love running around naked."

"And the first?"

Hands shaking, she yanked his jeans and shorts down his legs. "I love sucking your cock."

He closed his eyes and let out a long moaning sigh that grew louder as her lips closed around him.

She knew he must be primed from their lap session, and she was right. It didn't take long before he was bucking and panting, then rumbling his release. This time she managed to drink every last drop, without letting any escape.

When he grew soft, she released him and sat back on her heels, offering him a gamine smile.

He gazed at her with a blissfully dazed expression. "For limited oral experience, you sure know how to suck a man dry."

"Is that a compliment?"

"Hell, yeah."

* * *

After eating dinner in the nude, Kelsey challenged Sebastian to a newly devised game of Naked Scrabble, wherein players must kiss, lick, probe, or stroke a spot on the opponent's body beginning with each letter placed on the board. Needless to say, there were a lot of made-up words containing the letters 'p, b, a, d, and c' on the board by the game's end. Even though there was no clear winner, Kelsey declared herself the victor since she'd had three orgasms and Sebastian hadn't had any.

Sebastian humbly conceded defeat, then took his beautiful challenger for a victory lap in the bedroom.

Chapter Ten

Kelsey awoke to the smell of bacon and fresh coffee. Her stomach immediately rumbled and she stretched lazily, enjoying the feel of the cool clean sheets against her naked skin.

When she opened her eyes, she saw Sebastian standing in the doorway, again wearing only a pair of boxers, and watching her with an appreciative grin. His hair was wet, as though he'd recently showered, and his golden eyes sparkled with energy.

"Good morning, sleepyhead," he drawled. "I was just about to wake you."

"Good morning," she yawned. "What time is it?"

"About ten."

"Oh my goodness!" She sat up straight. "How long have you been up?"

He shrugged. "A while."

"Sheesh! I'm sorry I was zonked on you."

"You needed the sleep. I wore you out yesterday."

She smiled, remembering. "Yeah…"

"I kept busy. Fixed the garage door, mowed the lawn…"

"Mowed the lawn? I slept through the lawn mower?"

"I used the push mower—after I fixed it." He flexed his arms in a muscleman pose.

"Show off…"

"Damn straight."

"And cooked breakfast too? You're pretty handy to have around," she said with a sexy grin.

"Have to make myself useful somehow." He returned the grin. "Come on. Come eat."

Her stomach rumbled again as she got out of bed. "Gladly," she said, slipping her robe over her arms. The house was a bit chilly this morning, or she might have forgone the robe altogether. "Smells wonderful."

In the dining room, Sebastian had already set the table with plates and glasses of juice. As she took a seat, he brought out a skillet and scooped a large omelet onto each plate. Then he dashed back into the kitchen to bring a plate of bacon.

"I am thoroughly impressed. After the blender-coffeemaker incident, I was sure you were a stranger to the modern kitchen."

"Pans and heat sources have been around a while. It's the kitchen 'gadgets' I have trouble with. Kids of this era only have to know how to work a microwave—and I can do that."

"But once upon a time, you were a Guardian when modern appliances didn't exist?"

He nodded. "I was a Guardian when this country was still a British colony."

Her mouth dropped open. "You said a couple of days ago that you don't know how old you are because Guardians don't have years. What do you mean by that?"

"Guardians exist on a totally different plane of reality than regular humans."

"Different plane? Like another dimension?"

He nodded. "It runs parallel to this one, doesn't intersect, but it's close enough that elementary magic can get us back and forth."

Kelsey thought back to her mathematics classes. "Like two sheets of paper, one above the other?"

"Exactly. They're close, but they never touch."

"Does your plane have a name?"

"Thear."

"That's clever." She grinned, obviously catching the anagram of 'earth' immediately. "So you have a different time scale than on this plane?"

"Yes, because of magic. We don't absolutely require food or sleep, so the time between assignments on *this* plane is... amorphous. We can tell you that we had a break, and what we did during the break, but we have no concept of time having elapsed. That's why Guardians measure time in assignments, because it is only on this plane that we have a true concept of time."

Kelsey tilted her head and nodded. "Astonishing as it may seem, I actually understand. I'm amazed."

Sebastian watched her draw circles on her empty plate with her fork. He couldn't remember ever telling a human the things he was telling her, and he wondered why he felt she should know. Why hadn't he given her his stock 'Because we're magic' answer?

"Are there other beings besides Faerie Guardians in Thear?"

"Certainly. We have cities and countries and continents just like you. Guardians are a relatively small portion of the population."

"What or who are the other portions?"

"In my country most of us are Guardians, but some have different specialties—like tooth retrieval, or toy manufacture, or human relationships." He realized he hadn't answered her question exactly, but she didn't seem to notice, only laughed but didn't comment.

"Do you have a home?" she asked.

"I have a living space, but I wouldn't call it a home. I'm hardly ever there."

Her expression grew apologetic. "Oh! I'm sure it

would be okay if you wanted to spend time at your place, wouldn't it? I mean, I don't really require the attention your younger charges do, so I'm sure you don't have to stay here every day."

He shrugged. "It's a place to call mine, but not much for actually spending time in. I'd rather stay with you." He tried to muster a lecherous smile, but sex was not the reason he wanted to stay—though it was a big draw. Being with Kelsey felt very much like home, but he couldn't allow himself to examine that notion too closely, nor grow too attached to it.

"I'd rather you stay with me, too," she said quietly, then took a long drink of orange juice and set her empty glass loudly on the table, as though to distract from her admission.

Sebastian wasn't distracted, though, and his heart thundered in his chest. Did she feel the same?

"What happens to Guardians? I mean when they're done being guardians?" She moved her glass in a small circle, making a larger wet spot on the table.

He tried to search her face but she didn't raise her gaze to his. "It rarely—" He cleared his throat around a sudden lump. "It rarely happens, but... They're stripped of their magic and memory, and given a new existence and new memories."

"New existence?" Now she did look at him, her eyes full of question, her expression otherwise unreadable.

"As a normal human on this plane of reality. The way I understand it, former guardians wake up in a home they recognize, with a job they know they have, but with a bit of a gap in the memory department. But they soon settle into normal human life and enjoy a normal human existence for the rest of their days."

She circled her glass some more, seemingly lost in thought. After a few moments she grinned and looked up at him. "Do they get to keep their umm... well-endowed bodies?"

He laughed. "Yeah. Why?"

"I wonder if the job they know they have is in the adult media industry." She winked as she stood to carry their plates to the kitchen.

"I doubt we'll ever know, but it's an interesting idea."

Together they cleaned up the kitchen—he'd made a bit of a mess, not being used to cooking. He could have used magic to clean it up, but it was more fun working beside her.

When they were done, Kelsey filled a pitcher and went around the house watering plants while Sebastian sat at the table and watched. Then she dumped the remaining water in the sink, washed the pitcher, and set it in the dish drainer.

By the time she returned to stand beside him, Sebastian had long been considering the fact that she was naked beneath her robe, and that perhaps today was a good day for her to be the sex goddess she described yesterday.

"You have that look in your eye."

"What look?" he asked, offering her an innocent smile.

"That 'I want to fuck you senseless' look."

He pulled her into his lap and absently tweaked her nipple through her robe. "I'm just thinking about all the things I want to do to you, and the ways I want to do them. How do you feel?"

"Delicious," she teased, wiggling her hips so that she rubbed against his erection.

He molded his hand to her breast, and stroked the other hand down her back, over the curve of her hips, to cup her bottom. "Mmmm, I concur," he said, giving a gentle squeeze.

"What sort of things do you want to do to me?"

"I want to fuck you senseless… in naughty, inventive ways."

She stuck out a sassy lip. "I'm afraid I don't know what you mean. You'll have to show me." Her voice at once teased and dared.

"Do you trust me, Kelsey?"

"Absolutely."

"You know that all you have to do if something is too overwhelming is say 'stop' and I will."

Wariness mixed with excitement in her expression, but her gaze remained steady as she nodded.

"Are you ready?"

Kelsey grinned, almost too horny to bear. "Drenched." Whatever Sebastian had planned, she knew without a shred of doubt that he would never intentionally injure her. She had no doubt, however, that he would fuck her senseless in naughty inventive ways. Her body quivered slightly at the thought.

"First I have a few things for you." He put his hands behind his back and brought forth a black leather corset.

She gasped, feeling an immediate rush of warmth in her pussy. Her fantasy! She stood and eagerly shrugged out of her robe. "Oh Sebastian! Help me put it on!"

He did, helping her situate the garment comfortably around her ribs, then lacing it snugly, but not too tightly. The leather was buttery soft, held rigid with boning sewn into the seams. Metal rings skirted the bottom edge and attached in other various places, and she could only imagine what wicked purpose they might serve. The half-cups lifted her small breasts, making her nipples jut out sharply.

"The nipples of a sex goddess," he whispered almost reverently, teasing them with his thumbs until they tightened into painful pebbles.

Her pussy throbbed with excitement and she wriggled impatiently under is assessing gaze.

"Sit down so I can help you put your shoes on."

"Shoes?" She gasped as he knelt and picked up a sparkling silver stiletto heel from the floor beside her. She sat—the corset holding her upper body rigidly upright—and watched him carefully fasten the straps around her ankles. Then he stood and helped her to her feet, holding her hands until he was sure she had her balance on the towering four-inch heels. Kelsey veritably giggled. "Gina would call these Fuck-Me shoes."

He chuckled low in his throat. "Then today they shall be aptly named."

She turned in a little circle. "Do I look as sexy as I feel?" Because god she felt sexy!

"I could eat you up." His grin was wicked and sexy.

"Oooh, please do."

"One last item." He now held up a velvet blindfold. "This is where *my* fantasy starts."

She didn't hesitate. "I'm ready," she said, which was a serious understatement. She was very near orgasm already and he hadn't even touched her! But she waited patiently while he adjusted the blindfold over her eyes.

When it was secure, she felt his shoulder at her middle and found herself folding in half, down over his back as he lifted her in the air. "Hey!" She gave a token wriggle and thumped his muscular back with a fist.

He chuckled. "Your ass looks cute hoisted in the air like that." He turned his head and gently bit her thigh with a growl.

"Uhnn..." she groaned, feeling her pussy lips swell and gape. Her heart thumped steadily in her chest, seeming magnified by the confinement of the corset. Damn she wished she could see *his* cute little ass from this angle, and considered taking a quick peek, but remembered he was still wearing his boxers.

She sensed when they entered her bedroom, and when

he came to a stop, lunged slightly forward and began to lower her, she knew he was putting her on her bed. Her head and shoulders came to rest on a pillow as he arranged her on her back. She could feel her nipples pointing straight up, as the partial cups of the corset held her breasts upright. It was an odd feeling, and she brushed her hands over the hard peaks without thinking.

"Lift up your hips," he urged.

She did, planting her feet on the bed, spiked heels digging into the mattress, and levering herself up. He quickly slid a pillow under her ass and she lowered herself again.

"Good girl," he crooned. Then she gasped as he planted a wet, suckling kiss on her aching clitoris.

She cried out, then moaned her disappointment when he didn't linger.

"Patience, love. I'll satisfy that pretty pussy in a minute. I just have a few more details to…tie up." He straddled her body so that he was kneeling over her chest, then pulled one of her hands from her nipples and stretched it up and out. A furry cuff closed around her wrist, and she understood.

She had to laugh at the pun, but at the same time her pulse quickened in an exhilarating mixture of fear and excitement.

She felt him bend his head down to hers. "These cuffs have a safety catch on them." His lips brushed her ear, his low sultry voice sending shivers of delight curling along her nerve endings. With a gentle hand, he guided her finger to the tiny latch. "You can release them at any time."

She nodded and he fastened her other arm in the same fashion. Again, he guided her finger to she safety catch, and she nodded again, this time more emphatically.

He shifted slightly on the bed and she felt something

smooth and warm nudge her bottom lip.

"Suck my cock, Kelsey." His voice was strained and breathless.

She smiled and opened her mouth wide, circled her tongue over the tip of his shaft, then lifted her head slightly to close her mouth around him. He groaned, a long shaking sound, as he gently moved his hips in rhythm with her devouring mouth.

"Oh god, love, good girl. Suck me hard, that's it. Yess…."

She wished she could touch him, but knew this must be incredibly erotic for him, watching himself disappear into the mouth of a bound and blindfolded woman. The knowledge that she was pleasing him, fulfilling his fantasy, made her chest swell with satisfaction and her cunt swell with need.

"Ohhh, too close," he moaned, and withdrew from her mouth. He climbed off the bed and wordlessly fastened cuffs around her ankles as well. But the cuffs apparently weren't secured to the bed, for she could still move her feet.

He moved away for a moment and she heard the faint sound of fabric sliding to the carpet—he'd taken off his boxers.

In her mind's eye, she saw his magnificent cock standing thick and ready, glistening with her saliva, gently leaning under its own weight like the Tower of Pisa. She licked her lips again.

Where was he, anyway? "Sebastian?"

"Yes, love?" She felt the bed dip under his weight, and heard a jangly bump as he set something down while he moved to the center, between her knees.

Before she had a chance to further consider the jangly bump, his mouth was on the inside of her knee, gently suckling and laving her skin. He worked his way down at an agonizingly slow pace. When she thought he would end her torment, he softly kissed her clit, then began suckling and laving up the inside of her other leg.

"Arrrhhh!" she growled in frustration, lifting her hips, but he only chuckled.

"Patience."

"Patience my ass!" Her voice echoed off the bedroom walls.

After a brief silence, he said thoughtfully, "Hmm… Maybe."

Her breath paused in her lungs and her heartbeat seemed to hang for a thrilling moment at the implication of his words.

Would he?

He chuckled again and stroked a finger through the juices that betrayed how incredibly hot and wet the notion made her.

Finally his mouth settled on her cunt, suckling and nibbling, his tongue stroking and probing, stealing all rational thought that might have happened into her brain. "Ohhhh yessss!"

She lifted her hips to grind against his mouth, panting and whimpering her pleasure. Amid her spiraling ascent, she vaguely noticed that while he fondled her with his tongue, his hands worked at the cuffs on her ankles. But the thought was forgotten when she hurtled forward over the edge of ecstasy and tumbled back to her body.

"I so love to watch you come, Kelsey. You're so beautiful."

"Uhhnh…" she managed as her body continued to twitch.

"Are you ready for more?"

She nodded enthusiastically. With her vision hampered, other senses seemed to magnify, and she was acutely aware of the accelerated pace of his breathing. Whatever he was about to do, it excited him more than usual, which in turn heightened her own arousal.

"Tell me if this is too uncomfortable. The corset may pinch." As he said this, her feet lifted, apparently attached to either end of a long dowel or rod—likely the source of the jangly bump. Up and back, he lifted her feet until they were almost even with her hands. "Does that hurt?"

She shook her head. The corset boning *was* digging into her abdomen, but not enough to be painful. "I'm fine," she said.

Sebastian used lengths of rope to secure the dowel about a foot out from the headboard. Then he sat back on his heels and looked at Kelsey trussed up for his pleasure. Her blonde hair stuck out from the blindfold, making wild electric designs on the pillow. Despite the pull of gravity and her arms being bound out to the sides, the corset held her breasts in place, pointing to the ceiling, like tiny mountains inviting his mouth to climb. Also pointing to the ceiling were the dangerous-looking heels of those decadent 'Fuck-Me' shoes.

The position made her hips tilt upward, her swollen labia and anus ripe and accessible.

He leaned forward and kissed the back of one knee, his hands skimming the skin of her hips and ass. "So many ways I could pleasure this beautiful pussy, Kelsey." He let his mouth drift down to the back of her thigh.

"I could ram my cock into it until you scream my name with your climax. Would you like that?" To illustrate he laid a hand over her mons and delved his thumb into her dripping sheath.

She moaned and nodded.

"Or I could fuck you with my tongue while my fingers explore what's behind this pretty little flower." He moved his thumb down and rubbed her juices in a circle over her anus.

Her moan was a bit more impassioned as she tried to rock her pelvis against his hands.

"Or how about I fuck you with my fingers while I ram my cock into this velvety hole." He plunged his thumb past her sphincter.

"Oh god, oh god that feels so good," she cried, raising her hips even more.

Sebastian groaned too, becoming so hard it hurt. His teeth bit gently into her thigh as he fought for control. He'd suspected the last option would make her hot, and every fiber of his being wanted to do it, most especially his dick. But no woman had ever allowed him to take her that way before, and he wanted to make absolutely sure Kelsey was ready for it when he did. He didn't want to hurt her as a result of his own inexperience.

Making a decision, he withdrew his thumb and leaned over the side of the bed where they had stashed the blue box.

"What are you doing?"

"Shhh. Patience." He selected another dildo from the box, this one larger than the one they used yesterday—and purple. The base tapered slightly from top to bottom, so that at the bottom it was nearly as big around as his cock. Grabbing the tube of lubricant, he sat up.

And grinned again at her gaping pussy. "I love your ass tilted up this way, Kelsey." He drizzled lubricant over her anus, then put the tip at the tight opening and squeezed.

She hissed in a moan. "Are—Are you going to fuck my ass?"

"Sweet saints," he grunted, her words nearly sending him over the edge. He could hear the dark hopefulness in her voice and gritted his teeth. "Not today, love. Let's see how well you take a bigger dildo before I go ripping you apart."

Just then he had an idea, and a second after that, he'd

implemented it, using magic to produce a harness fastened about his waist. Securing the lubed-up dildo into the harness below his balls, he lifted his hips and guided it to her slippery flower, pressing gently.

"Oohhhhhhh, gooooood," she moaned as he pressed the big purple penis slowly into her ass.

"It's the purple one, Kelsey. Have you ever used it like this before?" He watched in fascination as her nether-hole opened around the dildo, stretching toward the bottom.

"Noohhhhhhh, god that hurts so good!"

Sebastian's cock twitched and he gripped it with his lubed hand, stroking in time with the motion of his hips, fucking Kelsey's ass with the dildo.

She jerked at her bindings, arched her back as she sobbed, "Yes! Oh god *yessss!*"

He couldn't contain his own groans of pleasure. A distant part of his mind wished Kelsey could see him, and he imagined himself from her point of view, looking at him through her raised thighs, seeing himself pumping his cock with his hand while his hips plunged the dildo home. "Oh god." He quickly let go of his cock before he spurted.

"Sebastian…Ohhh, I'm so close! Harder!"

But he had a better idea. He wanted to be inside her when she came, so without altering his rhythm, he leaned over, threading his upper body through her thighs, and guided his shaft to her cunt. As he plunged inside, he ground himself against her clit.

The new angle of his hips also changed the angle of the dildo, so that it didn't fully penetrate her. She arched her body against him after only two thrusts.

"Ohgodohgodohgod!" she cried as her internal muscles began to spasm mercilessly around him. He imagined what it would feel like to be inside her ass when she came hard like that, gasping and quaking,

Miraculously, he held on to his own orgasm until hers had subsided, then began to move his hips faster in and out, now fucking her with both dick and dildo.

"Ohh, Sebastian…"

He dipped his head and clamped his mouth over one nipple, suckling brutally. Soon his hips were slamming into her and she was gasping for breath.

"Oh no… oh no, not again," she cried. "Oh shit I'm coming, I'm co—oooaaahhhh!" The last word disappeared in a primal moan as she arched her shoulders forward, her body starting to quiver violently.

He felt his own release sweep over him as her cunt milked him again, and again, their orgasms seeming to stretch for minutes on end, drawing out his as well.

When he could move again, he reached up and depressed the safety latches, one by one, on first her ankles and then her wrists. Then as her arms and legs closed around him, he removed her blindfold.

Her lashes were wet, her gray eyes glittering with moisture.

"Did I hurt you?" he asked, alarmed. He brushed her hair out of her face and kissed her eyes.

"I—I don't think so."

"Why are you crying?"

She shook her head, then brought his face down to hers for a fierce kiss. "Thank you," she whispered.

"It was my pleasure."

She bit her lip and grinned. "I have to pee."

He laughed and carefully withdrew both himself and the dildo. She immediately scrambled off the bed and dashed to the bathroom, leaving her heels beside the bed.

When she returned, he had taken care of the purple dildo and the harness and lay on the bed. He motioned for her to join him, then pulled her against him so that he spooned her.

Though he was sated, he was still semi-erect, so he slid inside her slick folds once more and stayed there, unmoving.

They lingered in her bed all day, cuddling and talking, listening to the sounds of the day, of the kids playing in the neighborhood.

"I've never taken woman in the ass before," he confided toward late afternoon, and he heard her soft intake of breath. "No woman has ever let me."

"Have you ever wanted to?"

He nodded. "About as much as I've wanted to tie a woman up and have my way with her."

"You've never done that before either?"

"Not like that. Not with feet, too." He lifted himself on an elbow so he could see her face. "Did you enjoy it?"

"Yeah, very much." Color tinged her cheeks. "And not just because I knew you did. It was unspeakably erotic to be at the mercy of your pleasure."

He settled back into the pillows and waited, knowing her mind would return to the start of the conversation, to the subject he knew fascinated her. He was right.

"I want you to…take me that way…in my ass."

He grinned into her hair. "I will… but not today."

She nodded. "Tomorrow?"

"Eager?"

"A little."

"Maybe."

When her stomach growled, he used magic to produce a chicken salad sandwich, and she ate dinner for the first time in her life while impaled on a stiff cock.

Then he made slow sensuous love to her until they were both exhausted and drifted off to sleep.

Chapter Eleven

"Kelsey, José came in late and left early today. He said you already okayed it." The front office secretary twiddled her fingers. "Hi Sebastian."

"Hello," he nodded politely.

"No problem, Jenny. I told him not to come in at all, actually." Kelsey and Sebastian had just emerged from a meeting with Alonso Hargrave, a government regulatory agent. Fortunately he'd only had good things to say.

Sebastian had observed closely, playing the part of the St. Louis representative to a tee.

"The mayor called, and Miss Novak is in your office."

"Thanks, has she been waiting long?"

"About three minutes. I told her you were almost done."

Kelsey found her best friend sitting in the chair behind her desk, curiously looking through the stack of messages on one corner. Kelsey stood in the doorway, hands on hips. "Ahem," she said, and laughed when Gina nearly jumped out of her skin.

The other woman surged to her feet, hands thrown dramatically in the air as Kelsey stepped into the office. "Oh Jeezus, you scared me." She came around the desk wearing a beige blazer and miniskirt, a plunging purple chemise that showed plenty of cleavage, and barely-there strappy heeled sandals that made her nearly as tall as

Kelsey. And as usual, her almost-black hair was pulled back into a sexy little twist, from which a myriad of strands had escaped to brush alluringly about her face and shoulders.

"Hi Sweetie," she said, giving Kelsey a quick hug. "I just had wonderful afternoon lunch with Aaron down the street from here, so I decided to drop in to—we-e-ell... Who is *this*?"

Behind her, Sebastian leaned casually against the doorframe. "Gina, this is my friend Sebastian Phate. Sebastian, meet my best friend since college, Gina Novak." Kelsey braced herself, watching Sebastian's face as he shook Gina's hand in greeting. Her friend was chesty and vivacious, accustomed to the company of gorgeous men who had a hard time resisting those fabulous breasts.

But Sebastian's gaze showed only polite interest as he shook her hand, and never once dropped to Gina's chest. Kelsey watched for a hint of the sexual conquest she so often found dancing in his eyes, but it wasn't there when he looked at her friend.

"Kelsey's told me quite a bit about you." He gave her a warm smile, then moved to sit in the client chair nearest Kelsey. Crossing his feet at the ankles, he leaned back and casually placed a possessive hand on her hip. A small action that no doubt spoke volumes to Gina, whose eyes were suddenly the size of dinner plates.

"Very pleased to meet you, Sebastian." She titled her head. "Um... Kels? I think I left my sunglasses in my car. Can you come out with me to get them?"

Kelsey laughed. "Sheesh, Gina. You could be a little more subtle."

Gina seized her hand and dragged her out of the office and down the hall toward the front entrance. Once they were outside, Gina stopped and spun to face Kelsey.

"Details, girl. I want details and I want them now.

112

You look thoroughly sexed and I can't believe you haven't already called me!"

"I look different?"

"Hell yeah! Look at you!" Gina waved her hands grandly, gesturing first at Kelsey's face, then down her body. "You look like a cat who swallowed a goddam canary!"

Kelsey looked down at herself with no little consternation. "And how is that?"

"Utterly satisfied, girlfriend. And I've not seen you look like that in years, or maybe *ever*."

Kelsey shrugged helplessly. "Okay, I should have called. I've been so tied up—"

"Tied up?! Holy fuck!" Gina's mouth gaped open. "He knows about your little blue box, doesn't he?!"

Kelsey's mouth dropped open. "How did you know?!"

"You said *tied up*!" Gina gave her a 'duh' look.

"I could have been speaking figuratively! It's a common expression."

"Not common for you, honey. You forget I've known you most of your adult life. If you're tied up, you're tied up. Otherwise you're just busy—" She chopped a hand in the air as though to stop herself from continuing. "Where did you *find* him?"

"Well… that's sort of a long, complicated story…"

"I've got time—" Gina glanced at her watch. "Shit! No I don't! I gotta get back to work!" She pecked a kiss on Kelsey's cheek and dashed to her car. "Call me! I want all the gory details!"

Kelsey waved as Gina got into her Camaro and drove off. Did she really look different? *Nahhh*.

She made her way back into the building, walked back down the hall to her office.

And smack dab into Sebastian's chest. She looked

up to find an odd expression on his face.

"Why were you looking at me like that?" Thankfully he stepped back so she could enter the office and close the door behind her.

"Like what?"

"Almost wary, when you introduced me to Gina."

She sighed. "I was afraid you'd go drooling on her. Most guys do."

He looked at her incredulously. "Are you serious?"

"Yeah, she's always got a hot date with a gorgeous guy."

"No, I mean you seriously thought I'd be…interested…in her—if I may paraphrase?"

"Why not? She's a beautiful woman."

"As are you."

"Okay, but she's a sexy woman. Petite and curvy with perfect breasts."

"Kelsey, you are the sexiest woman I have ever met."

"Well I'm glad you think so. But you already know my story."

"I think you don't give yourself enough credit. I suspect guys would go drooling on you, too, given the chance. What did you tell me? Aversion to mediocrity? How many guys have you *let* drool on you?"

She lifted a shoulder and nodded reluctantly. "Okay, point taken."

"If I didn't know how thin the walls are in this place, I'd remind you what your sexy body does to mine."

"I guess it wouldn't do to have an employee—or client—walk in on the executive director *flagrante delicto* on her desk." She stuck out a pouty lip.

"Any appointments on the upper floors of tall buildings?"

"Unfortunately not. My only appointment today was with Hargrave. The rest is just a lot of paperwork. Wel-

114

come to my world. Telephone, meetings, paperwork." She sighed. "*All* my appointments this week are in one- or two-story buildings. Dammit."

He echoed her sigh and sat down heavily in a client chair. "Your friend is definitely quite a character. Likes to talk with her hands, doesn't she?"

"Yeah. She jokes that it's the Italian in her, but her mother is Puerto Rican and her father is American mutt." A thought occurred to her. "How did you know?"

"What?"

"That she likes to talk with her hands. She was only in here for a couple of seconds."

Color crept into his cheeks. "I peeked."

"You spied on us?" She grinned incredulously.

His chin lifted with exaggerated indignance. "I call it covert observation."

"Uh-huhh…?"

"I was curious to see how you interact with her."

She eyed him suspiciously. "Why?"

"She's your best friend and apparently knows you better than anyone." He leaned closer. "Does she always kiss you?"

"Yep." Kelsey grinned, suddenly knowing where this conversation was headed. A rush of heat flooded her panties. "Kisses me *and* buys me rubber schlongs, but the answer to your next question is no."

"No what?"

"What you're about to ask. I can see it in your eyes."

He grinned. "Have you ever thought about it?"

"Why?"

"Just curious." He looked furtively at her chest, where she knew her nipples had tightened painfully in her bra. Surely he couldn't see that, though!

She coughed a bit to cover her embarrassment. Then she sighed and twirled her hair. "The notion has crossed my mind—but not seriously." Her pussy throbbed between her legs. Why was this conversation making her so hot?

"That's what I thought." His eyes smoldered, and she knew he was imagining her and Gina together.

Oh! She couldn't stand it anymore! If they didn't get out of here soon, she was going to drag Sebastian under her desk, thin walls or no.

She stood abruptly and stuffed some papers into her briefcase. "Tell you what. I can take some of this paperwork home."

Sebastian didn't say a word, didn't even grin with triumph, merely stood and moved to the door. His eyes, however, continued to smolder, and she could feel his hot gaze on her as she retrieved her purse from the bottom drawer and came around the desk.

When she met him at the door, he pulled her against him and gave her a searing, teasing, mind-stealing kiss.

His erection pressed into her belly and she whimpered, her own sex almost painfully aroused as well. "Let's get out of here," she said, her voice weak and needy. Sheesh, she was a slut for Sebastian!

He opened the door and they nearly sprinted for the exit. On her way out of the building, she called to Jenny in the admin office, "Jenny, I'm heading out an hour early. If anything comes up, give me a call."

"Roger that," Jenny called back as Kelsey followed Sebastian out the door.

"I'll drive," he said when they had nearly reached the truck.

"*Can* you?"

"Give me the keys." His voice was hard, with an edge she found equally scary and exciting.

She handed him the keys.

He got in and moved the driver's seat back as far as it would go, then started the truck while she got into the passenger seat.

They had barely left the parking lot when he asked, "You have anything important in the back?"

"No, just a pair of galoshes, why?"

He turned the truck into a gas station and headed to the garage-like structure behind it. "I think it needs a carwash."

"What?" No! She wanted to go home and fuck him silly! She knew her voice sounded panicked, but she was *surely* going to spontaneously combust if she didn't get him inside her soon!

"Trust me."

He pulled to a stop and rolled the window down, then punched some numbers into the control box. When the light flashed green, he rolled the window back up and pulled forward into the bay.

Then he slammed the truck into Park, undid their seatbelts and pulled her into his lap. "I need to fuck you *now*."

"Oh thank god," she breathed with relief, and quickly moved to straddle him, situating herself between him and the steering wheel.

Before the machine had even started the pre-soak, she had hauled up the front of her skirt and he had yanked open the fly of his jeans, pulling himself free of his boxers. Then he nudged the crotch of her thong aside with the head of his penis and slammed into her. Two feral moans echoed in the small confines of the truck's cab.

Kelsey bounced up and down on him, arching her back, vaguely aware of the sprayers outside the truck now spitting suds. More immediate in her awareness was Sebastian and his thick cock inside her. "Ohhhhh," she groaned, gritting her teeth against the intensely desperate pleasure. Her fingers dug into his shoulders, his mouth suckled her breast through her blouse, as his hands gripped her hips and moved her up and down his shaft.

Already she felt herself hurtling closer and closer to release with each stroke as the felt-fringed scrubbers beat the outside of the truck with a thunderous roar. Sebastian gripped her hips tighter, quickened his pace, grunting with the exertion. Her own cries grew higher in pitch, more fervent, rising above the din of the carwash, until suddenly she took flight, gasping as the climax tore through her body, radiating out from her full, pulsing cunt to the very tips of her hair.

"Sweet saints!" Sebastian roared, and hammered his hips into hers, his body jerking slightly as his hot seed pulsed into her.

Her own body quieted and she slumped against him. As they gasped for breath, she noticed that the scrubbers had stopped spinning and now the rinse sprayers quietly deluged the vehicle, making the foam soap run down the windows like rivulets of semen.

"I'm so glad you're partial to wearing skirts to work," he said, his voice gravelly.

She grinned and raised her head. "Me, too. I can't seem to control my baser urges around you. It was a conversation about Gina, for crying out loud."

"And it made you as hot as it made me. I'm sure this is not a news flash, but you're just as horny and depraved as I am."

And what am I ever going to do without you? her heart cried. But she pushed the thought away as soon as it appeared. Then she noticed the gold sedan sitting at the control box, waiting for the carwash. "We'd better get a move on before that guy in the car behind us gets irate."

He gave an exaggerated sigh and flexed himself inside her. "I guess you're right. I can wait for round two until we get home."

With a shiver of anticipation, she lifted herself off of

him as he put himself back together. Then they both buckled their seatbelts and Sebastian pulled the truck forward out of the carwash and headed towards home.

* * *

Sebastian sat on the floor in the living room, in front of one of Kelsey's two large bookshelves. While she sat at the table doing her paperwork, he'd been keeping an eye on her, waiting patiently as he kept himself busy alphabetizing her books.

After arriving home following the carwash session, he'd decided to let her get her work finished before he monopolized her evening. But he'd had to find something tedious to do in order to keep his mind off of his raging desire to explore every explorable orifice of her body.

She had a wide variety of books, ranging from physics to history, literature to nutrition. He picked up the book atop the stack nearest him. *England Under the Norman and Angevin Kings, 1075-1225*. He smiled and put it on the shelf, then picked up another. *The Elegant Universe: Superstrings, Hidden Dimensions, and the Quest for Ultimate Theory*. No wonder she had no trouble with the parallel plane concept.

Finally Kelsey gathered up the paperwork, enclosed it neatly in a manila folder, and slid it into her briefcase.

"You finished?" he asked hopefully, quickly placing the rest of the books on the shelf.

"Yep. And I'm getting hungry."

"Literally or figuratively?"

"Yes."

"What do you normally do in the evenings when you get home from work?"

"Hmmm… My usual routine is… Read the mail, eat a protein bar, do ten or fifteen minutes of strength or resistance training, then five miles on the treadmill, eat, shower, watch the news, and go to bed."

He got a protein bar and a bottle of water from the refrigerator. "Eat this, go do your workout and I'll make dinner. Then I guarantee I'll satisfy the other hunger."

She nodded thoughtfully. "I like the sound of that."

* * *

Kelsey stepped into the kitchen about an hour later, her mouth watering at the delicious aromas. She peeked over Sebastian's shoulder as he stood at the stove. The meat in the pan surprised her though. "Salmon? I don't remember buying salmon."

He offered a sly smile. "Must have been in one of those mysteriously appearing bags."

"But it's very expensive—"

"Expense means nothing to me, Kelsey."

"But I feel badly eating so lavishly when others are eating macaroni and cheese."

"Well don't. I'm a Faerie Guardian and it's my job to pamper. I've been appallingly lax in my duties the past few days, but I need to do my job. And you deserve some just desserts. When I'm gone you can be as self-depriving as you want."

She sighed, appreciating how well Sebastian had already pampered her. "Okay… I guess."

"And that goes for other stuff, too, like laundry and cleaning house. I want you to have as much free time as possible." He served up two plates and gave her a wicked grin.

When he put it that way…

They ate rather quickly, blandly discussing the earlier meeting with Alonso Hargrave, both eager to finish the meal and move on to other activities.

As Kelsey was putting her dishes in the dishwasher, the phone rang. She gave Sebastian a smoldering look and picked it up. "Hello?"

"I didn't want to wait until you were too 'tied up' to

call."

Kelsey had to laugh at the urgency in her friend's voice. "Hi Gina. You called just in time. Three more minutes and you would have been too late."

"Is he there?"

"Yes…" she looked into the living room, where Sebastian was pulling DVDs off the small rack. "I think he's alphabetizing my DVD collection."

"Alphabetiz—Never mind. I won't ask. So who is he? Where'd he come from?"

Kelsey decided to stick with the story Sebastian had given Benji. "He's a counselor from Saint Louis. He came down to… to learn about the programs at Sophie's Wings, like the backpack program."

"And he's staying with you?"

"For a while, yeah. You know us public service types. Can't afford luggage, let alone a hotel."

"Why didn't you tell me he was coming?"

"Well… I didn't really know… the situation would be so…"

"Sizzling?"

"That would be an excellent word for it."

"How long is he staying?"

"I'm not sure. Until his superiors call him back, I suppose."

"So he tags along with you to work and observes, then makes fabulous love to you the rest of the time?"

Kelsey grinned in spite of herself. "That about sums it up."

"Girlfriend…I'm almost jealous."

"Well don't be. It's a temporary thing. I'll be back to my semi-chaste boredom in no time." Kelsey managed to keep her voice light, but the thought created a heavy lump in her chest.

"Then enjoy it while you can…"

"Oh, I am, believe me."

"…and don't do anything I wouldn't do."

"Is that possible?"

Gina gave an exaggerated sigh. "Okay, I guess not, but be careful, okay? Don't get too wrapped up in this guy if he's not gonna be sticking around. I don't want you to get hurt."

Too late, Kelsey thought, but said instead, "Thanks, hon. I'll do my best."

She said goodbye and hung up. And sighed. How was it that she'd become so attached to Sebastian in four days? Was it because she'd been so sexually deprived and Sebastian so thoroughly scratched that itch? Perhaps it was his magic that attracted her, or his willingness to please her in any way?

She shook her head, knowing it was none of those things. Sebastian fit her perfectly, physically, emotionally, intellectually. And if she wasn't careful, she might just fall in love.

"You okay?" Sebastian's hand slipped around her waist.

"Yeah. That was just Gina."

"You look pensive."

She gave a half shrug. "Daydreaming."

"Mmm…. What about?"

"About your guarantee."

"Oh?"

She glanced at her watch. "I think it's time for some just desserts."

He grinned. "I think you're right."

Chapter Twelve

Sebastian grabbed a can of whipped cream from the refrigerator, then swept Kelsey up into his arms and carried her down the hall to her bedroom.

"What's the whipped cream for?" she asked, giggling.

"For dessert, of course."

When he placed her on the bed she was naked, her clothing having disappeared into a poof of pixie dust. Sebastian's clothes followed, and as he opened her nightstand drawer to retrieve the cherries, she somehow knew he would give her the dessert she really wanted, the one they had talked about yesterday afternoon.

Then she would have to thank him in advance.

She pulled him onto the bed and pushed him onto his back until he was propped on his elbows. "Dessert for me first," she said, and squirted a ridge of whipped cream down the length of his cock. He gasped softly at the cold sensation, but she continued, adding two swirls on his balls. Setting the can aside, she picked two red cherries out of the jar and placed one atop each swirl of whipped cream as he watched.

Sitting up straight, she grinned at him. "Looks like I've made a *banana* split!"

He groaned at the corny humor, but lifted his hips. "I want to watch you eat it."

With a sexy smile, she closed her mouth over one white swirl and sucked both cherry and testicle into her

123

mouth. "Mmm…" she said, licking him clean, then pausing to chew and swallow the cherry.

She repeated the action on the other side, aware of Sebastian's gaze on her, watching her every move with rapt attention and smoldering gold eyes.

The second cherry eaten, she concentrated on the 'banana'—she groaned inwardly at her own terrible humor—and slowly licked the whipped cream from his skin. Then she took him into her mouth, letting him slide far back into her throat, and used her lips and tongue to clean up all remaining traces of whipped cream.

As she sucked him, she reached between her own legs to slide a finger over her hard button.

"Oh god…" he moaned and she saw that his heated gaze was now on her hand.

Smiling around him, she spread her pussy lips with her index and ring finger while she circled her middle finger over her clit.

"Oh god, Kelsey, yes…" His fingers laced in her hair as his hips began to buck and twitch. His gaze darted between her mouth and her masturbating hand, his groans becoming more impassioned, his thrusts becoming faster, deeper.

Finally he fell back onto the bed and roared as he spurted himself down her throat, his hips jerking upward with the spasms of his release.

When she had sucked every last drop from him, she released his cock and licked her way up over his washboard abs to his left nipple, and then on to his mouth.

His eyes sparkled and he grinned as she kissed him. "You stole my thunder."

She knew he was referring to her acting on his whipped cream and cherry idea, but she purposely misunderstood. "You'll have it back in a few minutes."

"Did you come?"

She shook her head.

"We'll have to remedy that." He rolled with her until she was under him. In one smooth motion, he sat up and moved down her body, grabbing the can of whipped cream as he did so.

She suppressed a giggle as he squirted a generous dollop on each breast, one on her mound, then a ridge running down over her labia to her anus. Then he dropped a cherry on each dollop. "Oh!" she gasped when he nudged a fourth into her vagina.

He grinned as he set the jar of cherries aside. "I'll refrain from spouting corny puns."

"Oh, come on. Don't I look good enough to eat? Aren't you aching to pop my cherries—into your mouth? " She stuck out her tongue and wrinkled her nose. "I'll bet you can't wait to taste my sweet cream."

She was rewarded with a painful groan—and the sight of his cock slowly, but surely, swelling back to life.

"See? Your thunder's already coming ba—youch!"

He bit her nipple with a growl, voraciously sucking cream and cherry into his mouth, along with her entire breast. Not at all gently, his mouth pulled on her flesh, tugged at her pebbled nipple until she arched with pleasure.

When she was panting and whimpering, he switched to the other breast, giving it equal brutal attention.

"Oh god," she cried as the stimulation made her ache with need.

His teeth raked down her body, over her belly, to her pubic mound. Fingers dug into the flesh of her hips as he lapped up the whipped cream and cherry.

She bucked and keened as his teeth nibbled her clitoris before he moved his mouth down to swirl his tongue into her cunt and then over her anus. Roughly his tongue assailed her, removing every last sweet trace, then delved into her sheath to suck out the cherry.

It was too much. Gasping, panting, moaning his name, she came, hard and fast, wave upon wave crashing through her body.

He continued to suckle her as her body quieted. Then before she could even grunt encouragement, he raised himself onto his knees, turned her over onto her stomach, and pulled her hips up to meet his forward thrust as he plunged into her.

As he pounded into her, she felt something warm drizzle over her ass, and she realized it was lubricant. Her heart leapt. When he pressed first one finger, then two, into her nether-hole, she moaned, a low guttural sound.

Too soon her orgasm rocketed through her and she sobbed his name, her arms and legs trembling beneath her, as he gradually slowed his pace.

When the spasms had subsided, he withdrew and pulled her down to the mattress with him, enclosing her in his arms, kissing her temples, cheeks, chin, as she struggled to catch her breath.

His cock nestled between her thigh and his, damp with her moisture, and still hard as a rock.

"You didn't come."

He shook his head, eyes blazing his intent. "I want to come in your ass," he whispered darkly.

The words nearly sent Kelsey into another orgasm, and she moaned, scorching need flickering and unfurling low in her belly. "Do it."

He growled, exhaling hot steamy breath against her neck as he pressed her back into the mattress and moved over her.

Lifting her ankles over his shoulders, he nibbled the insides of her knees.

Anticipation coiled tightly, painfully in her stomach. *This is it, oh god this is it.*

He gently squeezed more lubricant into and over her nether-hole, massaging with his fingers.

Oh god this is it!

"Are you ready, Kelsey?"

She nodded enthusiastically, unable to find her voice. She panted slightly as his tip pressed against her anus, and second thoughts flitted through her head. *He was too big. She was too small. She wasn't ready.* Fortunately third thoughts weren't far behind. *Oohh, that feels so goooood.* Her eyes drifted closed.

"Open your eyes, Kelsey, I want to make sure I'm not hurting you."

With tremendous effort she dragged her eyes open, and met his molten gold gaze. When he had her attention, he pressed a bit harder, and she bore down until she felt her muscles opening around him.

"Tell me to stop if it hurts."

Slowly he pressed inside until the head of his cock was inside her. "Uhnnhhhhhhh," she moaned, teetering on the edge between pleasure and pain, as she stretched wider than she had ever stretched before.

He pressed further and she hissed, the pleasure-pain almost unbearable. "Yesss, Sebastian. Oh god that hurts so good."

Further still he pressed, filling her, the sensation unlike any she'd ever experienced. Her pussy wept with moisture and she felt perilously close to the edge of release, yet pleasantly sated at the same time.

"Oh fuck, Kelsey. You don't know how good this feels."

Sebastian struggled to keep his own eyes open, but he worked hard to concentrate on her face rather than the exquisite sensation of his cock slowly entering her ass.

Finally he had slid in to the hilt.

"Are you okay?"

"Yeah." She gave him a somewhat dopey smile. "Feels amazing."

He watched himself slowly slide out of her, until the ring of her sphincter gripped the head of his cock. Then he pushed back inside, watching his dick disappear into her anus. *Sweet saints, he was fucking her ass!*

Hot satisfaction burned through him, and he increased his pace, sliding in and out with ease now.

She pulled her knees down to her chest and bent forward so she could see. "Ooooh, god, that's good," she breathed, then lay back against the mattress and tilted her hips to meet him.

"Touch your clit."

"What?"

"Touch yourself, Kelsey. Do it."

She reached a hand around and brushed a finger over her sensitive knot. "Oh god!" she cried as electricity zinged out to every nerve ending in her body.

"Go on," he grunted.

Carefully she spread the moisture from her empty cunt up over her clitoris and massaged gently, moaning as powerful jolts of pleasure radiated out from between her legs. Without warning her body shot heavenward, higher and higher, until she seemed to bounce and bubble near the peak of a powerful orgasm, and almost, almost, *almost* plunged over the edge.

"Fuckfuckfuckfuck," Sebastian growled, then hunched his shoulders and groaned, his hips grinding into her ass with each brutal thrust.

"Sebastian!" she screamed, the hot spurts of his orgasm pushing her over the edge into hers. She arched off the bed as it gripped her, holding her prisoner for long moments before crashing violently through her body.

She felt his arms wrap around her, heard her name whispered over and over near her ear, but it was a long time before she regained her senses.

When she did, she found Sebastian propped on his elbows above her, looking at her intently. He was still buried deep in her ass.

"Are you okay?" he asked, his voice tinged with concern.

She managed a smile. "I'd say you fucked me senseless."

* * *

Tuesday and Wednesday passed much the same way as Monday. They somehow made it through to early afternoon without ripping each other's clothes off, then rushed home to relieve a day's worth of pent up need. Working alongside each other without getting naked was exceedingly difficult, though they did manage to make it all the way home before succumbing to their more primal urges.

Tuesday evening was spent very similar to Monday evening, though with chocolate syrup instead of cherries, and Wednesday evening was looking to be even more entertaining.

But as they were clearing dishes, the phone rang.

Sebastian headed for the DVD rack, but Kelsey wasn't long on the phone.

"That was Jenny. She says firefighters are just putting out a blaze at the Sunny Retreats retirement home across town. I need to go."

"Wait, I'm going with you."

She smiled. "I thought you might. I'm going to throw some jeans on. Can you be ready to leave in five minutes?"

He grinned. "I'm ready to go now."

"I'll meet you in the truck."

True to her word, they pulled out of her driveway less than five minutes later.

"Did she say how bad the fire was?"

"Only that no one was hurt. She also said José had already picked up the van, so he'll meet us there."

"He sure is working a lot for having the week off."

"I don't know that wild horses could keep him away."

Kelsey gave him directions as they navigated through waning rush-hour traffic, and soon Sebastian was pulling the truck to a stop a block from the retirement home. He could see dozens of residents sitting in folding chairs and wheelchairs across the street from the still-smoking building.

They had just gotten out of the truck when a familiar white van pulled in behind them, and José jumped out.

"What are you doing here, young man?" Kelsey scolded.

José grinned sheepishly. "Dia made me. She said I was 'hovering' too much. I grabbed some cases of water and cookies from the warehouse. Don't know how much help that will be, but it's something."

Kelsey wrapped her arms around the younger man and gave him a quick squeeze. "You are such a blessing."

Sebastian suppressed a ridiculously sharp stab of jealousy. Even though José was married with a new baby, he was the kind of man Kelsey truly admired.

They walked in silence to where the residents sat watching firefighters. Fortunately the fire was confined to the west wing, leaving the east and north wings of the building untouched. Already employees had opened doors and windows to dissipate the smell of smoke.

Kelsey pulled a staff member aside and asked about the plan for temporary housing.

The large woman, whose nametag read 'Althea Watson, R.N.', smiled wide and accepted a bottle of water from José. "A few of our residents are on oxygen, so they'll spend a few days in a respite hospital just to be safe, along with anyone else who wants to go. The majority, though, would rather stay here, I think." She pointed to the damaged portion. "Firefighters have already sealed off the entire west wing with several layers of heavy gauge plastic. We'll close the windows in the rest of the building and fire up the air sanitizing units in a little bit, so at least the air inside will be smoke-free."

Kelsey nodded. "Let me know if there's anything more Wings can do."

"Will do, hon."

Kelsey turned to Sebastian. "Would you like to help us distribute cookies and water?"

"Of course. I'm here to help."

Minutes later, arms loaded with cases of water, he followed Kelsey and José as they handed out water and cookies to residents, staff, and firefighters. Sebastian watched Kelsey interact with everyone, how she paused now and then to offer a sympathetic ear or comforting hug, smiled encouragement to exhausted workers, and periodically checked with the fire chief for updates.

And when the water and cookies were gone, and the chief had given the go-ahead, she was the first to don her galoshes and venture into the blackened building, intent on rescuing treasured photographs and trinkets for the residents who couldn't do it themselves. And he was behind her every step, marveling at her compassion and commitment.

Two hours later, sooty and smelly, they headed back to her truck.

As they walked, Sebastian filled her in on what the fire chief had told him. "It looks like the fire started in a private bathroom, but investigators will be out tomorrow morning to have a good look in daylight."

"I'm just glad no one was hurt."

"For as much damages was done, it's pretty amazing." Sebastian looked around. "Where's José?"

"He left after we'd handed out water and cookies. Wanted to get back to Dia and the baby."

"Do you think Dia really made him?"

"Not a bit. I think Dia gave her blessing, but he was here because he's a good man with a big heart."

He opened the passenger side door and held it open for her, then went around to get behind the wheel. "How come he's the only one who came? I mean why not Benji, or even Jenny?"

She shrugged and looked out the window. "I don't know why the others don't come—maybe they know someone else will take care of it, but I can guess why José does. He's been on the receiving end of Wings' disaster relief cookies."

"Oh really?" He glanced at her as he pulled the truck onto the street.

"About ten years ago, he was a teenager, living in a small apartment with three younger brothers and his disabled mother. Faulty wiring sparked a fire that destroyed almost the whole complex. Everyone got out safely, and Wings was there with emergency supplies. My dad and I handed out hot chocolate and chicken soup. He made sure his mother and brothers got some, then helped us distribute blankets and diapers to the rest of the residents. He's been with us ever since."

"I hate to admit it, but I really like him, despite the fact that he laughed at my suit."

"I think he'll make a wonderful executive director someday, but don't tell him I said that."

He smiled, relieved to know she didn't intend to do her job forever, and hoping she gave it up before she, too, worked herself into the grave. "I think you're right."

She sniffed the air in the truck. "Whew. We stink."

"I'd say we smell like a job well done. You were amazing."

Color tinged her cheeks. "You helped a lot, too," she pointed out. "Thank you."

"All I did was carry water."

"And find Mrs. Turner's reading glasses."

"Yeah…" He grinned, remembering the old woman's gratefulness. A nurse had offered to buy her another pair, but Mrs. Turner had desperately wanted her old pair because her dead grandson had given them to her. So Sebastian had sifted through charred dressers and singed bedsheets to find the pair of glasses miraculously intact. "It was a wonderful experience. I've never had the opportunity to have a positive impact on so many people before, Kelsey. Normally my attention is focused wholly on one child. It feels amazing."

"It does, which is why I love my job, even though it's exhausting. Gina teases me sometimes about having a Masters Degree and making so little money, but she doesn't really understand that I get paid in other ways, too."

It occurred to him, somewhere in the depths of his consciousness, that he could help innumerably more people if he *remained* with Kelsey. While he'd spent centuries helping one child at a time, Kelsey had spent more than ten years helping hundreds of people at a time. If he could help her help them, perhaps she could reach more children and families—and maybe have more time to spend at home. If only he could stay…

* * *

Kelsey managed to get the key out of her front door lock only a modicum of struggle, and she tossed her keys and purse onto the dining room table. Sebastian closed the door behind them.

"Did I tell you how amazing you were tonight?"

"I believe so. Did I tell you how much you helped?"

"Probably, I don't remember. I might have been too distracted."

She narrowed her eyes, knowing full well he wasn't distracted during that conversation. "Distracted by what?"

"The thought of your naked body all soaped up in a hot shower."

She looked down at herself. "I am pretty dirty, aren't I?"

He growled his appreciation. "And I lo—" He bit the words off and buried his face in her neck to cover his near-flub. He'd very nearly said 'love you for it,' but that would have been a heinous mistake. *Temporary assignment, pleasant diversion, itch-scratching and all that,* he reminded himself.

Bullshit. Who was he kidding? There was nothing temporary about his feelings for Kelsey. The fact that he couldn't imagine his life without her scared the hell out of him, but he knew they'd both be better off if she didn't know that, and if he tried to forget.

"I wouldn't have you any other way," he said, setting troubling thoughts aside. He gave her a wicked smile and pulled her down the hall toward her bathroom. "Now let's get cleaned up so we can get *really* dirty."

"Mmmm…. You're on." She dashed ahead of him and turned the water on, and was shimmying out of her clothes by the time he got there. Within seconds their sooty clothes lay in piles on the floor and they stepped into the hot spray, closing the door behind them.

Chapter Thirteen

The following morning, she found him in the kitchen, pouring coffee into her travel mug.

"You recovered?" he asked when she slipped her arms around his waist from behind.

"From the fire call or from the shower?"

"Yes." He grinned and turned in her arms, his own arms coming around her.

"My arms are a bit sore, but I don't know if that's from lifting fallen beams or from hanging from the shower door."

"Probably a little of both." His lips brushed hers. "What's on the agenda for today?"

"Well, this morning I have two meetings downtown, then I need to go over to the warehouse to look over the month-end inventory. Then I have some phone calls to make at my office, and another meeting this afternoon."

"Business as usual," he said, brows furrowed. "You work too hard."

"Well, until we hire another Resource Director, I'll have to agree with you."

"Any applicants so far?"

"Nope—Oh sheesh! I almost forgot! Tonight I have to go to a charity benefit dinner for Sophie's Wings. Would you like to come?"

He grinned, but thankfully didn't voice the alternate interpretation she could see dancing in his eyes. "I want to go wherever you go, if it's all right with you."

She accepted the mug when he handed it to her. "Of course it's all right with me. But it's formal dress. You'll have to wear a nice suit or tux—a *dark colored* suit or tux."

"I think I can manage that. What about you? What are you going to wear?"

"Me? The usual. I have a dark gray sparkly knit thing I usually wear to these functions."

"Did you wear it last year?"

"Yes. So what?" She preceded him out of the kitchen and set the mug by her purse.

"How about this one?"

When she turned, he stood next to her holding a black velvet gown on a hanger. Silver sequins undulated in sparkling waves, contrasting the mute softness of the fabric.

"Ohhh! It's so beautiful!" She stroked a hand longingly down the dress, then shook her head and let out a regretful sigh. "No."

His brow furrowed. "But you love it."

"I know, I *do*, but I can't."

"Why ever not?"

"I don't draw a large enough salary from Sophie's Wings to be able to afford something like this, and I don't want anyone to think I do."

"So tell people I bought it for you."

"I hate to lie, Sebastian."

"But you'll do it when necessary."

"I wouldn't consider my evening wear *necessary*."

"I like that idea even better."

She couldn't help but smile. "Do you ever think of anything else?"

"Not when I'm around you."

"I'll be fine wearing my knit dress."

Sebastian shrugged, somewhat disappointed, and

hung the dress in her closet anyway.

* * *

Sebastian tagged along with Kelsey to her morning meetings—meetings that were usually the responsibility of the Resource Director. By now she usually invited him to join her, rather than make him sit in the waiting area.

Then they headed to the warehouse where Kelsey went over the accounting and inventory while Sebastian helped José fill backpacks for delivery tomorrow.

Back at the office, he mastered the fax machine with Jenny's help while Kelsey made phone calls and met with a stern-looking woman wearing orthopedic shoes.

At about four-thirty, Kelsey found him in the admin office.

"You ready to go?" she asked, her eyes flashing hunger like a lighthouse.

His 'thunder' stirred in his jeans. "Whenever you are."

"Jenny, we're headed out."

"Aye, aye, Captain."

He followed Kelsey out of the building. "Interesting meeting?"

"Boring as hell. My mind kept wandering."

"Her shoes made you hot, didn't they?"

She laughed. "Oh yeah. It's a little-known fetish." They got into the truck, buckled, and she backed out of the parking spot. "But somehow memories of a steamy shower were more interesting that the orthopedic shoe fetish."

"I can't imagine why." He grinned. "Shoes are much more exciting than my dick sliding in and out of your tight pussy while you finger your ass."

"Oh god. Okay, we have to talk about something else now."

"There's a carwash," he teased, pointing out the window.

She grit her teeth and focused on getting home. Good lord, when had she become such a nymphomaniac? Yes, Gina had always teased her, but something about Sebastian made her insatiable, her body needing him inside her as often as possible.

After what seemed an eternity, she pulled the truck into her driveway and bolted for the house, Sebastian only steps behind. The front door opened as she reached for it—sometimes Sebastian's magic was a godsend. She quickly tossed her purse and keys into an easy chair, kicked off her shoes and pulled Sebastian down onto the couch with her.

He fell heavily on top of her, but she didn't care. Her hands tugged at the hem of his green silk t-shirt, pulled it over his head. His hands pushed her shirt and bra up over her breasts and his mouth fastened on a nipple.

She barely noticed the urgent grunts and moans that filled the air—she concentrated solely on the need to get Sebastian inside her. He dragged her skirt up her legs and she arched against him, reaching for his zipper as he rubbed against her, deftly releasing his cock, then pushing his jeans and shorts down over his hips.

Every inch of her body flamed with need, her desperate sounds of urging matching his. Rough fingers clasped her hips and he shoved inside with an urgency she greatly appreciated. She cried out his name in relief as he began to thrust with feral abandon, quickly launching her into the stratosphere.

* * *

Later that evening, Sebastian found Kelsey bent over the dining room table, transferring essentials from her regular purse into a small pearl-studded clutch purse.

She was wearing the dress.

His loins stirred at the sight of her ass, hugged perfectly by the snug velvet. And he could only grin when he

138

saw that she was wearing the stiletto 'Fuck-Me' heels he'd given her.

She stood and gave him a dazzling smile. "What do you think?" she asked, turning slowly so he could see the full effect. "I tried it on, just to see…and couldn't force myself to take it off in favor of the knit thing."

A strange noise emanated from his throat, and he had trouble swallowing. He realized his mouth was hanging open, but somehow couldn't form a clear thought geared toward closing it. The black velvet shimmered in subtle waves, while the sequin accents seemed to undulate over her curves in a sweet caress.

She'd pulled her hair up into an elegant twist, but several strands had escaped to brush her neck and shoulders. She had applied a hint of makeup to her face, smoky gray around her eyes that made her own gray eyes sparkle and seem larger. Her full lips were dabbed with a dusty red hue.

"You like?"

He nodded dumbly, still unable to find his voice.

She tilted her head to one side. "You okay?"

Again he nodded. Then he blinked and cleared his throat. "Speechless is all," he managed to say. "You look absolutely stunning."

She beamed. "You look delicious yourself." Her gaze fell to his crotch, and she reached out and adjusted his dinner jacket over his erection. "If we didn't have to be there in three minutes, I'd take care of that for you." She licked her ruby lips and winked.

"Uhnnn," he groaned as he allowed her to pull him out the front door.

Fifteen minutes later, they walked into the lobby of the Holiday Inn, longstanding site of the yearly gala.

They had no sooner cleared the doors, however, when Jenny and a photographer pulled them aside and positioned them in front of two large green urns.

"Pretend it's prom!" Jenny bubbled.

"Three, two, one—Smile!" the photographer cried, then snapped the picture.

Kelsey blinked at the spots before her eyes. "I didn't know we were going to have a photographer."

"Oops. I guess I forgot to tell you," the other woman blushed. "It was my idea. When we had so many people purchase tickets this past week, I thought it would be good to have a photographer here. He's doing this for the profit on portraits."

Kelsey smiled. "Good thinking, Jen."

The photographer handed Sebastian a card with a number on it. "Your picture will be ready after dinner."

Sebastian tucked the card into his breast pocket. "Thanks." Then he turned to Kelsey and held out his arm. "Shall we?"

She smiled, tucked her hand into the crook of his elbow, and they entered the ballroom.

"Why Kelsey Marie! Don't you look stunning! Heavens, what a *gorgeous* gown!"

"Thank you, Eugenia. You look equally dazzling." Kelsey paused to hug the gray-haired woman in a blue sequined gown.

"Why thank you, dear. You're so sweet. And who is this handsome young man with you?"

"Eugenia, this is my friend Sebastian Phate. Sebastian, this is Eugenia Parks, former Resource Director for Sophie's Wings Community Assistance. She retired last month after fifteen years of service."

"My, my. I don't believe I've seen a man look that good in a tuxedo since my Reggie married that NFL cheerleader." She put a hand on Sebastian's arm. "Reggie's my grandson, you know. Takes after his father. Such a pretty face, but hasn't got the common sense of a house fly."

"Eugenia!" Kelsey really shouldn't have been shocked, as Eugenia often spoke of her son and grandson in such terms. But not usually with total strangers.

"Oh, it's okay. Both of them have been fortunate enough to find good work flexing their muscles for those fitness magazines. That's one thing they're very good at— flexing their muscles."

Sebastian gave her a wry smile. "I find it hard to believe you're old enough to have a grandson getting married."

"Oh, you're so sweet. You look like you could be a magazine man, too. Do you model?"

"Not in public," Sebastian said enigmatically. "I work for a non-profit organization in Saint Louis."

"Oh? A man of service? I like a man who gives of himself."

"Then you would love Sebastian," Kelsey said, trying not to laugh.

"Edward." Eugenia tugged on a nearby portly man's elbow. "Edward, come meet this kind gentleman from Saint Louis."

Sebastian smiled politely as he was introduced to Edward Hopkins, then Diana Thomas and Leonard Bowdon, all members of the Board of Directors for Sophie's Wings.

After the others had drifted off to other conversations, Sebastian leaned down to Kelsey's ear. "Why did Eugenia retire? Couldn't she have stayed on until you found someone to replace her?"

Kelsey shook her head. "Her doctor has been telling her she needed to retire for a couple of years now. Two months ago he gave her an ultimatum: retire now or find another doctor, preferably one who specializes in post-mortem."

"Ah. I see."

141

"So I fired her." She waved at a former client.

"What?"

"Well…I offered her forced retirement. She was going to stay on anyway, told me she felt fine. But I'd really rather not have anyone else die on the job—Hi Benji." She stopped when her co-worker stepped in front of her, his eyes as wide as his grin.

"Oh Kelsey! That dress looks absolutely deadly on you! I've never seen you look so… so scrumptious!"

"Thank you. You look dapper yourself. Where's Gerhardt?"

"Oh, he'll be here shortly. Got held up at the office, then had to run home to get changed." He nudged Kelsey and nodded his head toward Sebastian. "The poor thing can't wait to get a look at your beefcake hottie." He winked, then stepped back again. "But wait 'til he gets a load of *you*!"

"Thanks, Benj. Hey, are José and Dia here? I want to see that new baby!"

"Yes, they're here, but I don't know where. All these people! I've never seen so many people at a banquet before!"

When Benji moved on, Sebastian laughed softly. "Who's Gerhardt?"

"Benji's life partner."

"Oh." He raised an eyebrow at the unexpected response.

"They're a very cute couple."

"I'll wager Gerhardt wears the pants in that relationship."

Kelsey just laughed and shook her head.

"What? What's so funny?"

"Gerhardt's a professional drag queen."

"No kidding?"

"Nope. He's a friend of Gina's actually. They were

in a few community theater productions together. It's how he and Benji met."

Sebastian laughed out loud. "That's too crazy."

"When you live a boring life, it helps to have exciting people around through whom to live vicariously."

"I had no idea you wanted to be a drag queen." He smirked, no doubt suppressing a chuckle.

"Of course not," she admonished. "Females are faux queens, not drag queens. And I'm pretty dang close tonight. Gerhardt will be proud—Oh! I think I see Dia!" She seized his hand and pulled him through the throng of people to where she had seen the younger woman, but she was gone by the time they got there.

"Is that her?" Sebastian pointed to a small dark-haired woman standing with José a few yards away.

"Yes! Thank you." They approached, and Kelsey slipped her arm around Dia's shoulder while José spoke with another man. "How are you doing?" she asked Dia.

"Oh my goodness! You startled me! Took me a second to figure out who this tall beautiful woman was."

"It's the shoes." Kelsey lifted the hem of her gown to show the four-inch heels. "You've not met Sebastian yet, have you?"

"No, but José has told me about him—Pleased to meet you, Sebastian," she said, shaking his hand.

"Wow!" José said when he turned and saw her. He had a tiny bundle cradled in one arm.

Kelsey held out her arms. "May I?"

"Sure!" José wrapped his free arm around her waist, giving her a quick squeeze. Then he stepped back and grinned. "*Oh*, you meant Reina..." He chuckled as he handed the baby into Kelsey's arms.

"Ohh! She's precious!" Kelsey crooned as she gazed at the sleeping baby in her arms. "Sebastian, look! Doesn't she look just like Dia?"

"Thank goodness," José joked.

Kelsey smiled up at Sebastian, who looked at her with an odd expression on his face. "Sebastian?"

He returned her smile, though it seemed almost wistful. "She is beautiful, and she does look like her mother."

Kelsey returned her attention to José and Dia, who looked appropriately elegant, José in a black suit and tie, Dia in a long gauzy purple dress. "I'm so glad you guys came, and brought your new sweetheart. You look great, Dia!"

Dia pointed to the skin under her eyes. "The miracle of concealer."

Kelsey laughed and carefully handed Reina to her mommy. "If you need a babysitter, let me know. She can come visit me any time."

"Better watch what you offer," José warned with a wink. "We may take you up on it."

"You know I'm good for it." She waved slightly. "See y'all later."

She and Sebastian milled around some more, chatting briefly, then moving on. Kelsey hated this part of the banquet, where she was expected to thank everyone for coming and comment on their contributions to Sophie's Wings. She would much rather find a quiet corner and watch people, but she accepted her responsibility as executive director, and reluctantly followed through on it.

"Would you like a drink?" Sebastian asked after they had left an elderly couple.

"Sure. Tea would be nice. Thank you." She offered him a sweet smile and he headed to the drink table.

"Hello Kelsey, you look fabulous!" Ellen squeezed her arm as she passed.

"Thanks, Ellen, so do you!"

"You look delicious, as always, Ms. Schroder."

Kelsey turned to see the familiar form of Bryce

Kirkpatrick, tall and lean, good looking in his own Ken-doll way. "Umm, hello, Mayor."

"That dress is very becoming on you."

"Thank you. It was a gift."

"From that man you're with?"

"Yes, as a matter of fact."

"Did you see the news last Thursday?"

"Umm... yes, actually. Benji called and told me to turn my TV on. I suppose we can thank you for the last-minute rush to purchase plates."

"It's the least I could do given all Sophie's Wings has done for the community."

"We do our best."

"I've left several messages for you."

"I know, I'm sorry. This week has been sort of hectic. My warehouse manager is working reduced hours—he and his wife just had a new baby. I've been handling Eugenia's workload on top of mine, and we had a retirement home full of fire victims to see to."

"You work too hard."

"So I'm told." With relief she saw Sebastian returning. However that relief dissipated when she saw the thunderous look on his face. He crossed the last few yards with slow deliberation, until he stopped beside her.

"Your tea," he said, carefully handing her an ice-filled glass. Then he folded his arms across his chest, letting the fabric pull taut across his wide shoulders and generous biceps, and gave the other man a coolly assessing glare.

The mayor drew himself up to his full height and returned the glare. Both men were roughly the same height, but Sebastian carried at least fifty more pounds of muscle, making the mayor look quite skinny.

"Sebastian, this is Mayor Bryce Kirkpatrick. Mayor, this is my friend, Sebastian Phate."

Kirkpatrick's eyebrow rose hopefully. "Friend?" he

145

asked, looking at Kelsey.

She glanced at Sebastian, who didn't look very 'friend'-ly at the moment. She ran a hand soothingly over his back, silently willing him to relax. "Sorry, he's—"

"Her lover," Sebastian finished.

The mayor looked again to Kelsey for confirmation. She thought about denying it simply because Sebastian was acting like such an oaf, but she could only nod demurely.

"I see," the other man said, quickly hiding his disap-pointment.

She handed the mayor her untouched tea. "Um, would you excuse us for a moment, please?" She didn't wait for an answer before she headed for the nearest door, towing Sebastian behind her. Once out of the ballroom, she led him to a door marked with both a man and a woman—a unisex bathroom. She pushed the door open to find an empty sitting area with a counter and mirror, and another door leading to the facilities.

Inside, she crossed her arms across her chest and faced him squarely. "What was that all about?"

He lifted a shoulder. "What?"

"The Neanderthal business with the mayor?"

"The man was undressing you with his eyes! He would have jumped you had I not showed up with your tea!"

"You're exaggera—" She looked at him suspiciously. "Are you jealous?"

"Hell yes!" His brows furrowed and he pulled her against him. "I don't want any other man even *thinking* about doing to you the things I've done to you."

She clearly felt his erection against her belly, caus-ing her body to respond immediately. "I'm pretty sure nothing so creative would ever occur to Mayor Kirkpatrick." She sighed as his lips brushed her jaw. "I'm

146

fully aware that Bryce has a crush on me, but I have absolutely no interest in him beyond friendship. He *is* a nice man, and I just don't want to insult him. He's a big supporter of Sophie's Wings."

"Well now he knows to direct his dick somewhere else," he grumbled near her ear.

"Sebastian!"

"What? You said you have no interest in him. Now he won't waste his time or yours showering you with unwanted attention."

She narrowed her eyes at him—even though he couldn't see her face with his mouth nibbling her neck. But she couldn't help smiling when she realized he'd probably done her a favor. "I guess so…" she conceded. And truth be told, it was rather exciting to see two powerful men posturing over her, no matter how ridiculous their behavior.

She heard the lock on the door turn, seemingly by itself.

"Sebastian?"

"Speaking of directing dicks…" He slid his hands around to her ass and began pulling up the skirt of her gown.

Her heartbeat kicked into high gear. "What are you doing?"

"Making the evening more exciting, and getting you off your feet." He lifted her to the counter and wedged himself between her thighs. His erection nudged intimately against her as his mouth found the sensitive spot beneath her ear, sending a luscious shiver spiraling down her spine and making her cunt pulse with anticipation.

"We can't do this here!" Despite her words, her hands worked desperately to unfasten the fly of his pants.

He chuckled against her neck. "Sure we can. You did ask me if I wanted to come."

"Why can't I resist you? One touch, one word, and I'm wet with wanting." Her voice sounded breathless and wanton to her ears.

He gave her a self-satisfied smile as she released his cock from his shorts and wrapped her hands around it. "I don't know, but I'm not complaining."

He tugged aside the crotch of her thong and pressed the head of his cock into her wet channel.

"Wait!"

He withdrew with a groan.

"Before we get too carried away…" She grabbed her clutch purse from the counter beside her, rummaged around in it, and pulled out a foil-wrapped condom. "Easier cleanup," she said and tore it open.

"You came prepared," he rumbled approvingly as she rolled the snug latex down his shaft.

"Better prepared than squishy."

Chapter Fourteen

Sebastian bit back a groan of longing as Kelsey allowed him to pull out her chair for her. With flushed cheeks and slightly swollen lips, she looked captivatingly sexy, and it was all he could do not to pull her into his lap during the main entrée to relieve the renewed hard-on between his legs. It was just a blessing they were sitting, so that his throbbing cock and tented pants were hidden. Boxer shorts weren't much for keeping stiffies under wraps.

Dinner was elegantly bland—he noticed Kelsey barely touched hers. He also noticed that her gaze frequently darted to his lap. He wondered if the state of his body had anything to do with the way she squirmed uncomfortably in her seat every now and then.

Between dinner and dessert, she gave a thank-you speech, detailing many of the things Wings had accomplished in the last year—thanks to the generous support of the people in attendance, and outlining plans for the next year.

Following dessert, Sebastian followed Kelsey out into the lobby, keeping her close in an effort to conceal his still-raging erection. The effort, however, proved to be counter-productive, since keeping her close only made him harder. Damn, that dress looked good on her!

"Do you want to see what the portrait looks like?" she asked.

"Sure." He followed her to the table, pretending not

to have forgotten, and fished their number out of his pocket. "We're number sixteen."

She picked up the appropriate envelope and opened it. "Ohh," she groaned. "You look great, but I've got a goofy grin."

He took the photo, which was actually two smaller images printed under a larger image, and looked. "That's not a goofy grin, it's a wonderfully bright smile."

She rolled her eyes and watched him put the photo back in the envelope, which he then put in his pocket.

As he stuffed a twenty-dollar bill into the glass jar on the table apparently for that purpose, a tall, thin man in an expensive suit approached with Benji.

"Kelsey! Oh my gawd! Look at that dress! Look at those *shoes*! Girl, add a three-foot wig and six pounds of makeup and you coulda walked straight off the stage at *La Cage*."

"I *am* feeling very glam tonight. I knew you'd love the shoes."

"Love them? I want a pair just like them! Do they come in larger sizes?"

"I'm not sure. They were a gift. Gerhardt, this is my good friend Sebastian Phate."

"I was wondering about this handsome fellow standing behind you." He held out his hand to Sebastian. "Very nice to finally meet you. Lord, where did you get those muscles?"

Sebastian shook hands with the man who looked like an average masculine guy—though perhaps a bit more flamboyant—and tried to imagine him in drag. Surprisingly, he *could*. "I'm blessed with good metabolism and lots of energy," he explained in answer to Gerhardt's question.

"I do hope our Kelsey is on the receiving end of some of that energy, eh?" He nudged Sebastian.

"Gerhardt!!" Kelsey and Benji both admonished.

"What? Honey, it's no secret that you're all work and no play. Gina's always complaining that you need to find a good male member." His gaze dropped meaningfully to Sebastian's crotch. "Goodness!"

Kelsey closed her eyes and waited for death by embarrassment, her cheeks flaming, her hair no doubt beginning to smoke. She felt Sebastian's hands around her waist, pulling her to him so that his erection pressed against her lower back.

"If you'll excuse us, gentlemen, I'd like to take Kelsey home for a good workout."

"Oooh, you go girl!" Gerhardt cheered as she allowed Sebastian to steer her toward the exit.

"It's nice that your friends are so supportive of your sexual exploits."

"Yeah, and it's sad that said exploits are so rare that it's a big deal when they happen."

* * *

She held him off until they were inside her house. Though she'd been tempted to let him take her in the truck, she wanted more than just a quick fuck like they'd had in the bathroom. She wanted to get naked and stay that way, and she had something else in mind.

And Sebastian was eagerly helping her reach that goal. He'd already unzipped the back of her dress while she fumbled with the key in the lock, and he now peeled it down her body. She had to toss her purse quickly aside in order to get her hand out of the sleeve. He held her steady while she stepped out of it, then tossed it on top of her purse, until she was standing in only thong, thigh-highs and heels in her front hallway.

His own jacket, tie and cummerbund had stayed in the truck, and he now shrugged out of his shirt as she opened his fly and shoved both pants and boxers over his hips, releasing his fabulous cock. She knelt before him and took him into her mouth, giving him one long languorous suck, while he kicked off his shoes and carefully stepped out of his pants with a deep tortured moan.

Then she stood and walked toward the bedroom, her heels clicking on the hardwood floor, her ass-cheeks swaying as temptingly as she could manage.

He hastily pulled off his socks and followed, completely naked.

When they were in the bedroom, she led him to the bed and shoved him gently down onto it. "Tonight I'm in charge," she told him, giving him her sternest look. "You are to call me only Mistress or Ma'am. You are not to use my name or any other term of endearment. You are to do what I tell you when I tell you to do it. No hesitation, no questioning. Tonight is only for me, and it is your job to satisfy me. Do you understand?"

Sebastian nodded, making a slight gurgling sound in his throat. Incredibly his cock swelled even larger under her severe gaze. She snaked the fingers of one hand into his hair and tilted his head up to look at her.

"Do you understand?"

"Yes, Mistress."

"Good boy." She retrieved the blindfold from the drawer of her nightstand and slipped it over his head. "Can you see?"

He shook his head.

"Good. Now move to the center of the bed."

He obeyed immediately while she dug the wrist- and ankle-cuffs out from under the bed.

"Spread your arms and legs."

Again he obeyed immediately.

She grinned and carefully secured his hands to the headboard and his feet to the footboard. When she was finished, he was moaning almost desperately through gritted teeth, his cock engorged and purple.

"Do you like being tied up, Sebastian?"

After a beat, he answered. "Yes."

"I'm going to relieve some of your urgency. I want you to come as quickly as you can, do you understand?"

"Yes, Mistress."

She climbed onto the bed and knelt between his spread legs, wrapped one hand around the base of his cock and gently cupped his balls with the other. She then licked up his shaft and took as much of him into her mouth as she could, and *sucked* like she knew he loved. His hips arched off the bed as he growled and panted, tugging at his restraints. Soon she felt his balls tighten in her hands, but she could sense that he was holding back.

She tugged aside the crotch of her panties and drew her right forefinger through her own copious juices, then gently pressed it into his anus. He yelled, part surprise, part passion, then erupted almost instantly, jetting semen down her throat, his sphincter muscles pulsing around her finger.

She swallowed every drop, then looked up at him without removing her finger from his ass. He wore a dazed smile on his face.

As she expected, his cock remained partially rigid, and would no doubt be fully erect again in a few minutes. She wiggled her finger in his ass and watched his shaft jerk. *No doubt*, she thought, withdrawing her finger.

Her pussy was dripping now, and she was close to her own release. So she crawled up the bed, nibbling and licking along the way, pausing to swirl her tongue around his flat nipple, then arranged herself over his face. Tugging aside her thong, she touched her nether lips to his mouth.

"Lick me," she commanded. "Lick me hard and long until I tell you to stop."

He lifted his head and stroked his tongue through her drenched folds. "Mmmm," he said, licking his lips. "I love your honey, Mistress."

A little shiver raced down her spine. "Good, now make me come and drink my honey."

He set to the task enthusiastically, alternating long strokes and concentrated suckling. She was wound so tightly that she felt her body reaching for release within minutes.

"Ohhhh, good boy, Sebastian. That's it."

"Mmmmm..."

She ground her hips into his face, tightened her abdominal muscles. "Almost... almost..." she panted.

He took her clit between his teeth and tugged gently as his tongue fluttered against it inside his mouth.

She had to grip the headboard as the orgasm crashed over her, fast and furious, but by no means intense. "Oh *yes*," she cried. "Good boy!" Just enough to take the edge off.

"Stop," she said, lifting herself away. She didn't miss the wicked grin on his face, and she knew he was thoroughly enjoying himself. She found further proof of his enjoyment when she moved back down his body and stroked a hand over his again rigid penis and gave it a quick kiss. "I knew it wouldn't take long. Your thunder is amazingly resilient."

He chuckled low in his throat. "I aim to please, Mistress."

"And that you do." She let her nipples graze the fine hairs of his chest as she moved up his body once more. Then she pressed her lips to his, tasted herself on his lips. His mouth opened and she delved her tongue inside, claiming him with her mouth as he had done to her countless times.

When they were both groaning with renewed pas-

154

sion, she drew back and pressed the middle fingers of her left hand into his mouth.

"Suck my fingers," she commanded, her voice breathless.

He obeyed, drawing on her fingers, sucking with such sensuous power that she thought there must be a direct connection between her fingers and her pussy.

"You are such a good boy," she whispered. "I think I'll let you watch now." While he continued to suckle on her fingers, she reached behind his head with the other hand and released the blindfold, then tossed it aside.

Sebastian opened his eyes and his golden gaze met hers. She sat transfixed, watching him suck her fingers, knowing he watched her face.

She finally withdrew her fingers from his mouth…and hesitated. She knew exactly what she wanted to do next, but she wasn't quite sure she had the courage to actually do it.

"What's next, Mistress?" Sebastian asked, his eyes speaking his encouragement.

She smiled and took a deep breath, then maneuvered herself off the bed. With an exaggerated bow that made her breasts jut out, she retrieved the blue box from beneath the bed. While he watched, she selected a thick butt-plug and showed it to him. She knew he would think it was for him—she wanted to make him sweat a little bit. His eyebrow rose, and a flicker of worry passed over his face.

"Do you trust me?"

"Implicitly…Mistress."

"Are you *sure*?"

"Yes, Ma'am."

"Good, but you don't have to worry. This isn't for you." She turned her back to him and shimmied out of her panties, bending low to slide them down her legs. The action gave him a great view of her ass and made her swollen pussy gape open. Then she stood and lubed up the plug. Bending over the chair so he could see, she very slowly shoved the plug into her body as she ground her fingers into her clit. "Oh shit," she sighed as a small orgasm washed over her.

He moaned in near-agony.

When she had taken the whole thing, she retrieved another toy from the box with trembling hands and straddled him on the bed again, this time facing his feet. Her pussy pulsed with anticipation, needing to be filled as full as her ass. Her nipples tightened painfully.

"Is that what I think it is?" he asked, tense amusement in his voice.

She held the big pink dildo up where he could see it before setting it on the bed again. "Yep. My second favorite penis."

"Second favorite?"

"This one's my most favorite." She gripped his big cock in her hands, held it perpendicular to his body, then impaled herself on it. He dragged in a ragged breath.

"Ooohhh," she sighed, and began to move herself up and down his shaft. With the plug in her ass, he seemed immensely bigger— One last thought occurred to her. "You are not to come until I tell you, okay?"

He arched his hips, meeting her downward movement. "Yes, Mistress," he grunted, almost desperately.

She couldn't see his face, but she was sure his eyes were on her ass, so she leaned forward so that he could see the black plastic of the base of the plug.

He tugged at his bonds, thrashing a bit beneath her.

"Don't come," she gasped as she felt her own orgasm approaching.

"Unnnng..." he groaned. His hips continued to slam upward, his cock filling her, propelling her closer and closer to release. She rotated her hips, ground her clit against him; her hands clutched his legs.

Rapture broke over her, washing down her body, and she cried his name. He merely held is breath and gritted his teeth until her inner muscles had ceased their squeezing.

When she came back to her senses and her body had quieted, she raised herself up on her knees, pleased that his cock was still rock hard when it slipped out of her, and maneuvered around to face him. As he watched, she shoved the big pink dildo into her cunt, then reached around to withdraw the butt plug.

"Oh god," he moaned as she settled herself over him again, then guided his cock, amply lubed with her own juices, to her ass. "Oh god, Kelsey. Fuckfuckfuck…" He gritted his teeth, visibly working to hold on to his restraint as he sank into her ass, filling her vastly more than before.

"Another fantasy," she breathed. "Double penetration."

His breath hissed between his clenched teeth.

She raised herself and rocked forward, felt him slide out of her, his thick shaft seeming to grate against the dildo inside her. Down and back, and he slid in again. "Oh god…"

The sensation was almost too much, too soon. Her body was primed from her recent orgasms, and another loomed large.

"Fuck my ass," she commanded as she leaned down over him, letting him slide almost completely out.

He didn't hesitate, raised his hips and slammed his cock into her, brutal in his assault, grunting with the effort of restraint. "Aauuugh shit Kels… I can't… hold back… much… longer."

"You can come! You can come!" she cried as she plummeted headlong into sensual oblivion.

He roared his own release, and she sobbed his name as his hot semen pulsed into her.

Her body completely spent, she collapsed twitching and shaking against him.

"May I free myself?" he asked, his voice breathless.

"Please do." She didn't have the strength.

In an instant his arms were around her, holding her fiercely against him. "A double penetration fantasy?"

She blushed, despite her fatigue. "Yeah, if I were a sex goddess for more than a day…except…both cocks real."

"You are irresistibly naughty."

"I do my best."

* * *

"That was some pretty hot lovin', Mistress Kelsey," he said a long while later, after he had coaxed three more orgasms from her body with his mouth, fingers, and pink dildo.

"Don't I know it." She snuggled against him, struggling to keep her eyes open. "Thank you for letting me play."

"It was my pleasure, I assure you." She could hear his grin in the darkness.

"Would you really have let me use the butt-plug on you?"

He was quiet for a moment, then said softly, "Yes."

"Really?" she asked, somewhat surprised. But not too surprised for a yawn.

"Yes." He said it this time without hesitation. "Though if given the choice, I would prefer to start smaller."

"Hmm. I think Mistress Kelsey might be able to accommodate that."

His chest shook with his amusement. "I imagine she could."

Thoroughly exhausted, Mistress Kelsey drifted off to sleep.

* * *

Gina poked her head into Kelsey's office. "Is Sebastian here?"

Kelsey placed the phone back in the cradle. "I was just trying to call you, woman—left you a message. Sebastian walked down to Taco Bell to get us something to eat."

"Good." She came in and flopped into a client chair. "Why 'good'?"

"He makes me drool with jealousy."

Kelsey laughed. "How was your hot date?"

"Don't ask."

"What?! I thought he was a perfect gentleman."

"He was."

"So what happened? Did you find out how he performs in bed?" Kelsey waggled her eyebrows with exaggerated lewdness.

"No, and it's your fault." She threw her hands out and let them drop, indicating frustration with Kelsey.

"*My* fault? How do you figure that?"

"Okay, you've always been excruciatingly choosy in your sexual exploits, where I've just been interested in a big warm dick attached to a reasonably muscled body with a nice face…. You with me so far?"

Kelsey wasn't sure, but she nodded anyway. "Mm-hmm…?"

"When I get wild, it's kinda ho-hum, fun for a few minutes, but I'm lucky to get an orgasm without working for it. But when *you* choose to get wild, it's that much more exciting, you know what I mean?"

"Umm…"

"I've never seen you look like this, Kels. You're freakin' glowing. And that's all I could think about as I sat there all through dinner before the game, just looking at him, saying to myself, 'I don't *like* perfect gentlemen! I need a guy who's edgy and dangerous, who takes what he wants, including me. So why would I even consider wasting my time on this guy?'"

"But—"

"Wait. How many orgasms did you have yesterday?"

"Umm…" Kelsey hedged.

"Come on, 'fess up. I'm trying to prove a point here."

"I don't remember exactly. Seven? Eight? Maybe more? Oh wait. Add one for the bathroom at the banquet."

"Holy fuck, Kelsey! Are you kidding me?!"

"Shhhh. No, but last night was an exception. Usually it's only four or five."

"*Five*? Damn, woman, I was jealous when I thought it was two or three. No wonder you're glowing." She chopped a hand through the air. "Okay. You've more than proven my point. *That's* why I couldn't bring myself to waste one perfectly good mediocre orgasm on a guy that did absolutely nothing for me."

"Are you going to see him again?"

"What's the point? I repeat: He does nothing for me."

Kelsey tried to look sympathetic. "I've got an unused gift certificate to Anya's Toybox if you need it."

"Shut up."

"Hello, ladies."

Gina glanced up as Sebastian walked in, then did a small double-take and winced. "Damn, I am so jealous! You don't happen to have a brother, do ya, Sebastian?"

"Uhh…sorry to disappoint you, but no."

"It was worth a shot."

"You want a chicken taco?"

"No thanks. I need to get back to work anyway." She leaned over the desk and kissed Kelsey's cheek, then stood and shook her head. "Four or five… Life is not fucking fair."

"Four or five what?" Sebastian asked when Gina had gone.

"Just idle girl-talk stuff. Hey, did you have any trouble

at Taco Bell?"

"Nope. And I brought you these."

Kelsey's eyes widened when he held out a vase full of pink lilies. "Ohh! Sebastian, they're beautiful! Why?"

He shrugged. "Because *you're* beautiful?"

"Thank you!" She set the vase on her desk and grinned up at him—no one had sent her flowers since high school, aside from her dad's funeral.

Sebastian set a chicken taco in front of her, along with a cup of Diet Coke.

"And thanks for going to get lunch."

"No problem." He returned her smile, then sat to eat his cinnamon twists.

Oh to be able to eat only what pleased the palette, and not have to worry about calories or nutrition!

When she had eaten her taco, she glanced at her watch. "Would you like to go with me to check on the retirement home residents this afternoon?" She deliberately phrased the question without using the word 'come.'

"Of course I would." He raised a knowing eyebrow.

* * *

Althea Watson, the same nurse from the other night, was manning the main desk.

"Hi, y'all! Thanks so much for your help the other night! Our residents really appreciated your help and concern."

"It was our pleasure. We just stopped in to see how everyone is doing."

"All are back in-house—fortunately we had a bunch of unused rooms so everyone still has their own space. It's just not the same space for some of them, and that can be distressing."

"Did they figure out how the fire started?" Sebastian asked.

Althea laughed heartily. "It turns out Mrs.

Erlichmann was smoking a cigar in the bathroom. She accidentally set the toilet paper on fire, which set the trash can on fire, which shot flames so high it ignited the wall above the tile and spread into the ceiling."

"Goodness! Is Mrs. Erlichmann okay?"

"Sure is. She bolted when the toilet paper first caught, except she didn't tell anybody for fear of getting in trouble for smoking."

"Somewhat ironic, isn't it?"

"She's now launched a one-woman anti-smoking campaign that she plans to develop and take to other retirement homes."

Sebastian grinned. "I say more power to her."

"Do you mind if I leave a few business cards?"

"Sure, honey! Leave a card, send some brochures, hang a banner for all I care. We have some very grateful families who might be willing to thank Wings with their wallets."

Kelsey took some business cards and a few brochures from her purse and laid them on the counter. "Even non-perishable food items would be greatly appreciated."

"I'll spread the word."

When they were outside, Sebastian expressed his admiration. "That was excellent public relations, Kels."

"Why thank you."

"What's next?"

"Nothing. José is taking care of backpack deliveries, and I passed my only two appointments off to Benji."

"So we're free to go home and make merry?"

She bit her lip. "Or make naughty…"

"I'll drive."

Twenty minutes later, Kelsey yanked the key out of the lock and turned to tell him what she wanted to do to him.

But right at that moment, his beeper went off.

Chapter Fifteen

Kelsey's heart and stomach plummeted to the floor as nausea and panic washed over her. Her purse and keys dropped out of her hands and hit the floor with a racket.

This was it.

Seemingly in slow motion, Sebastian looked at his beeper, then back up at her, his eyes filled with regret, sorrow, pain.

Through the din of crushing emotion she heard him say, "It's the *big* boss. Must be urgent…"

She choked back tears. "No," she whispered.

He pulled her into his arms, wrapped them tightly around her. "I'll… have my friend Gabe hook you up… with a good man who shares your interests."

"No…" She shook her head against his chest. "I don't want to be hooked up." The front of his shirt was wet and she realized some tears had escaped. "I wish I could have *you* forever."

"I wish you could, too." He hugged her close for long moments, neither wanting to let go. But his beeper went off again. "I've gotta go."

"I know."

He released her and stepped back, his hand giving hers a final squeeze. "Goodbye, Kelsey Schroder,"

"Goodbye," she whispered.

And he was gone. Kelsey watched the pixie dust settle to the floor. She'd known this moment would come.

She swore to herself she wouldn't get emotional, that she would just raise her chin and go on with her life, grateful for the experience.

But she'd been kidding herself. How could she raise her chin when her heart was writhing in pain on the floor? How could she not get emotional when it felt like a vital part of her had disappeared with Sebastian?

Tears brimmed at her eyes and she looked around, searching for something to do, something to distract herself. But there was nothing. Her house was immaculate, her lawn pristine. Her gaze fell on the vase of lilies, and she crumpled to the couch, the floodgates of tears wrenched opened.

Her house suddenly seemed empty, lifeless, and she didn't know how she was ever going to feel content here again.

She thought about calling Gina, to cry on her best friend's shoulder. Even though Gina had warned her not to get too attached, Kelsey knew she'd listen and empathize. But she didn't feel like talking now. Maybe tomorrow.

Kelsey checked the lock on the front door, then dragged herself down the hallway to her bedroom. Perhaps she could sleep the weekend away and wake up Monday morning feeling good as new.

Yeah right. She would probably spend the weekend at the warehouse, immersing herself in tedious and unneeded work, like re-doing inventory—anything to keep her mind busy.

Everything hurt. Her heart, her head, her clothes. Without thinking about it, she kicked off her pants and pulled off her shirt.

And happened to catch her reflection in the mirror.

What the ...? Her hands went to her chest, where her breasts bulged out of her bra—the bra that had fit fine when she'd put it on that morning.

She smiled through her heartache as she unhooked the now ill-fitting scrap of material and tossed it aside, freeing beautifully full and rounded breasts she'd never seen before. Sebastian had granted her one selfish wish, a departing gift she supposed. She ran her hands over them in a sorrowful daze, squeezed them together, lifted them in her hands to feel their weight. And then burst into tears again.

Anguish poured from her soul and she cried harder than she could ever remember crying. Not bothering to pull on a nightgown, she crawled into her cold empty bed wearing only her thong panties. She pulled Sebastian's pillow to her face and hugged it, inhaling deeply of his scent, then soaked it with her tears as it muffled her cries of grief. She stayed curled there, sobbing until long after she had no tears left, long after the sun had set, until sleep finally claimed her.

* * *

Sebastian stood outside the general's office, his chest feeling as though he were being slowly crushed to death. He wanted to be anywhere but here, to go feel sorry for himself and wallow in his loss. But more than anything he wanted to be back with Kelsey. He knew he couldn't return to his former existence, so he had two options. He could convince the general that his job should take on broader scope, or he could risk everything, leave it all behind and hope he could find her again.

A small photo appeared in his hand, the one they'd had taken at the banquet—was that only last night? Seemed like a lifetime ago now. He called an indelible marker to his other hand and carefully wrote her name and address on the back of the photo, then kissed it and tucked it into the waistband of his jeans. Even if he had to be discharged completely, stripped of his magic and his memory, he would find her again. He just hoped the photo didn't somehow get lost in the transformation. Perhaps he could get it quickly tattooed on after the meeting with the General. He'd need to talk to Gabe, too, in case he couldn't get back to her. He prayed he'd have time.

The door to the general's office burst open, and the general himself stood impatient and red-faced on the other side.

"Phate! What took you so long? Get in here and have a seat."

Sebastian entered but couldn't sit. "Sir, I have a request."

The general took his own seat behind his desk and pointed a chubby finger at one of the two overstuffed chairs opposite him. "Sit down. We need to talk."

"I believe I can be more effective—"

"Save it. You're being taken off active duty."

Sebastian's heart fell. He'd hoped the general might be open to re-evaluating Sebastian's job description. Failing that, he had only one other choice. He touched the fabric of his shirt over the photo in his waistband and his resolve strengthened. He'd get back to her whatever it took. *Please let the photo make the transition with me.* He took a deep fortifying breath and opened his mouth to request a discharge—

But snapped it shut again when he saw Gabriel Hart step into his line of sight.

* * *

Kelsey awoke feeling somehow perfectly contented. She caught herself smiling sleepily before she remembered that Sebastian was gone. Her world crashed down around her all over again, thudding steadily, and she groaned out her misery, knowing she would surely die of heartbreak. How could she get up and face the day like nothing ever hap—

Her pillow shifted slightly and the thudding increased its tempo.

Wait a minute, that wasn't agony thudding in her head…it was… a *heartbeat!*

She sat up and looked down at the bed beside her. Joy burst in her chest.

"Sebastian!" She squealed her delight and threw herself on top of his sleeping body, wrapping her arms around him, kissing his lips, his chin, his cheeks, his neck.

He opened one eye and grinned sleepily under her onslaught. "Hmmm…I could get used to waking up like this." He turned his head and caught her lips as she peppered his face. "I guess I fell asleep waiting for you to wake up."

"Why didn't *you* wake me up?"

"I tried, but you were out cold, clutching a soggy pillow." He smiled tenderly as he swiped a chunk of hair behind her ear. "Did you miss me?"

She felt like giggling, but held back her joy just a bit, afraid to feel too much relief. What if he would still have to leave again? "Are you… Are you here…?"

"To stay?"

She nodded tentatively, fearing his answer.

But he grinned wide. "I'm afraid you're stuck with me."

She squealed again, sounding very much like a seal in heat, but she didn't care. She squeezed him tightly and giggled, unable to contain the happiness that bubbled up from the depths of her being.

His arms came around her and he nuzzled her hair.

"Oh, Sebastian, I thought I might die, it hurt so much. Not just sad hurt, but real pain."

"Shh, I know. I felt it too."

"I don't ever want to feel like that again."

"I can't guarantee life will be pain-free, but I *can* tell

you I'll be with you through it all."

She gazed into his face, questions racing around in her head, not the least of which was, "How—?"

"A wish is a wish is a wish."

"What does that mean exactly?" She kissed his neck again, then his chest.

"Apparently a Guardian outside this profession was keeping track of how many times you wished…and decided to hook you up with someone who shared your interests."

Her gaze returned to his face. "Outside this profession?"

"In another field."

She giggled in spite of herself. "What do you mean? Pixie? Elf?"

"A Guardian specializing in human relationships."

"Cupid?"

He wrinkled his nose at the term. "I think he would cringe at being called that, but yeah."

"Is this the Gabe you mentioned?"

"Mmm-hmmm."

"So what did my wishing have to do with it?"

"Well, it seems there's a clause buried somewhere in Article 548, Section 1296, about anyone wishing the same thing seven hundred seventy seven times."

Kelsey blushed. Had she really wished that many times that a gorgeously muscled six-foot tall man would appear in her bedroom?

He cleared his throat and continued, his cheeks bearing a hint of color. "Apparently Gabe was also keeping track of the number of times *I'd* wished to find the perfect woman. Seems there's a similar clause somewhere in Article 672, Section 89."

That made her feel a trifle better, only she knew he'd had a lot more years to wish seven hundred seventy seven times.

"Why didn't you tell me about a letter?"

Kelsey thought back. "As I recall, I was about to, but someone's sour attitude distracted me." She kissed him on the nose. "What was important about the letter?"

"Do you remember who signed it?"

"J.R. Manning, or something like that."

"R.H. Mann?"

"Yes! That's it!"

"The letter was an information-gathering device."

"Umm...how's that?"

"When you held the letter, the magic contained in it gathered information about you and transmitted it back to headquarters."

"What sort of information?"

"Your likes, dislikes, desires, concerns, whether or not you were trustworthy...things of that nature."

"Why?"

"It was a test, believe it or not, a final deciding factor on whether or not I was assigned to you."

"I guess I passed."

"With flying colors."

"Okay, as long as you're explaining the unexplained, what about that warm bubbly feeling? You said you didn't do it."

"Turns out we both did." He stroked a hand over her hair. "I didn't know it at the time, but it was the Bonding."

"You know I'm gonna ask, so go ahead and explain."

"It very rarely happens, because Guardians so seldom mate while still Guardians. But apparently when Guardian souls mate, they create a particular magic—that feels warm and bubbly at first."

"Magic? And what do you mean by 'at first'?"

He rolled slightly and pressed her into the mattress with his body, tucking her beneath him as his hard cock nestled against her mound. "The magic I'll have to explain later, because I don't fully understand it yet myself, but I do know that we make it every time we touch, and especially when we *fuck*."

"I like the sound of that," she said, and rocked her hips against him as her hands slipped inside the waistband of his shorts.

"Thought you might." He raised his hips while she pushed his boxers over his hips and down his legs, then used her foot to drag them completely off.

That accomplished, she wrapped her hands around him. "So you do have a magic wand after all!" she giggled.

"Ohh, that was awful," he groaned, but his eyes danced with amusement.

She stroked him absently as another thought occurred to her, and she grew serious. "Did you have to give up your other magic?"

Something flickered in his eyes. Wariness? "If I did?"

"Sebastian…" She placed one hand on his cheek and looked into his eyes. "I love *you*, not your magic. All that matters is that you're here with me. I'll take you any way I can get you."

Relief swept over his features, along with a deeper emotion. His lips found hers, gently but urgently.

"God I love you so much," he breathed as his mouth left hers to nibble at her neck.

Kelsey's heart nearly leapt out of her chest and flew away at hearing the words. An exhilarating feeling, to say the least.

As his teeth sank into her shoulder, one hand lightly skimmed the skin of her hips before dipping into her thong to stroke her slick folds.

"Oh, god," she groaned when his finger brushed her swollen clit. Her hips bucked against his hand and her fingers dug into his back.

He growled into her neck and pulled his hand away. She whimpered at the retreat, until he grasped a side strap of her thong and yanked hard. The thin satin gave way immediately and he tossed it aside. Now he stroked her clit again, but this time with the head of his cock rather than his fingers, while his mouth skimmed the tender skin at the vee of her neck.

She moaned and arched against him, offering her breasts—but that reminded her…

"Wait a minute…" She rolled him back over and sat on his stomach again. "I noticed these last night." She lifted her large breasts in his hands. "Didn't you refuse my wish because my breasts were perfect the way they were?"

"Perfect breasts come in all shapes and sizes. I wanted to make you happy." His hands came up to knead and tease the subjects of their conversation.

"Thank you. I love them, I feel incredibly sexy."

"You've always been incredibly sexy. And I can always change them back."

It took her a fraction of a second to realize what he was saying—that he still had his magic, and she laughed. "Okay, I feel incredibly *outwardly* sexy, to match the vixen inside."

"Vixen is right," he said, then rolled her beneath him once more and surged into her pussy, filling her with his enormous cock.

Her screech of laughter quickly turned into a moan of encouragement as pressed the fleshy mounds of her breasts together and raked his teeth over first one peak, then the other.

But he didn't move his hips.

"Please, Sebastian…" She tried to rock *her* hips, but his weight held them immobile.

171

He sighed with exaggerated contentment as he buried his face in her cleavage. "Please Sebastian what?" he asked, the words muffled.

"Uhhhnnh!" She arched her back in frustration, needing more, much more.

"Please Sebastian what?" His body tensed and he lifted his head, a feral smile on his face. His eyes flashed, hot and molten, and she knew he was purposely teasing her.

"Please Sebastian fuck me hard!"

He sat back and flipped her over without preamble, bringing her up to her hands and knees. In front of her, the wall behind the headboard shimmered, and by the time she figured out the significance of that, she was returning his hot gaze in the mirrored reflection.

"I want to see those luscious breasts bouncing as I slam into you."

"Uhnnh…" She closed her eyes and moaned, both at his words and at the feel of his big cock pressing into her cunt once more.

"God I missed being inside you yesterday."

Kelsey didn't want to think about yesterday, didn't want to think about how much she'd missed him, too. Fortunately he began to stroke into her with long, pounding movements, which chased all extraneous thought away, so that she focused only on right now, and the sensations radiating from her pussy.

"Rrrrr…" he growled, and she looked at him in their reflection. His eyes were on her chest, where indeed her heavy breasts bounced and swayed with every hammering thrust.

With a sly grin, she raised one hand to massage the new abundance of her bust, pinching, squeezing and tugging the flesh for his eager eyes. Then she did something she'd never been able to do before—she bent her head and licked her own nipple.

"Fucking vixen," he ground out, and pushed a slippery finger into her ass.

"Oh my god!" she cried, her fingers digging painfully into her breast. "Oh god, Sebastian, uuhhnnnnh....more... Please..."

He added a second finger, then a third, pumping them in rhythm with his hips. "Oh god," he whispered.

Her body teetered on the edge of a shattering orgasm, ready to take flight—

She slid her hand down to her pussy and briefly tugged her nether lips before concentrating circling fingers on her clit.

"Kelsey...Oohhhhhhhhhhhh god!" Sebastian's body twitched, his pummeling fingers stiffened, as she felt his hot seed fill her.

All at once she shattered, falling violently into rapture. She sobbed as the orgasm claimed her body, mercilessly wringing her pussy, jolting through the rest of her body.

She felt Sebastian pull her against him and settle her into his lap, and she slumped backward against him. His gasping breath skittered over her neck, its pace nearly matching hers.

Holy fuck, she thought, borrowing a very Gina expression. *I get to have a lifetime of this.*

Sebastian noticed Kelsey's dazed smile in the mirror—and his own satisfied grin.

This felt nice. Buried to the hilt in Kelsey, her breasts more than filling his hands, her sated body limp against him. He could get used to this.

His smile widened with the knowledge that indeed he *could* get used to this.

"I love you," he said, needing to say it again.

"Yes you do." She squeezed her interior muscles

around him.

His cock twitched inside her, and a contentedly joy-ful laugh rumbled up from deep inside him, until it bubbled over. She looked worried for a fraction of a second before she, too, was laughing. He dropped one arm to wrap around her waist and hugged her to him. They fell to the mattress together and continued laughing until their sides ached.

* * *

"So what is the status of your... job?" Kelsey licked a bit of mustard off her bottom lip and took another bite of her sandwich. They had missed breakfast, and now she wolfed down a ham on rye, famished from her morning exertions.

"I'm no longer on official active duty." Sebastian didn't *need* food, so he sat kitty corner next to her, lei-surely picking at his sandwich. And enjoying the view—they sat naked at the dining room table.

"So you're kinda sorta unemployed?" She reached for a napkin.

"Kinda. The powers that be agreed that I could do much more good as an unofficial Guardian for all the clients of Sophie's Wings." He scooted his chair back and sprawled his legs out in front of him, his hands folded behind his head.

"Hmmm...It just so happens that we're looking for a Resource Director. I've noticed you're very good with directing..." her gaze dropped briefly to his dick "...re-sources. Do you have a résumé I could present to the rest of the Board?"

"Do you think you could stand working with me every day?"

"I think I could get used to it." The last bit of her sandwich disappeared into her mouth, and he watched her chew with rapt fascination.

"Do I get to deal with that exec at Palmer Foods who

couldn't keep his eyes off your legs?"

"Sebastian," she scolded playfully, giving him as stern a look as she could no doubt muster. "We can't allow personal grudges to interfere with the beneficial dealings of the organization."

His clutched his chest with mock affront. "When have you ever known me to be anything other than a perfect gentleman?"

She gave him a 'you-can't-be-serious' look. "Oh, I seem to remember some Neanderthal behavior at a recent banquet."

"To be fair, at the time I thought he might actually pose a threat to me, especially since I thought I would have to leave you forever. He's good-looking, powerful—"

"Self-centered, plastic, and pushy. He doesn't hold a candle to you."

"Now that I can stay, the Neanderthal will stay locked in his cage until someone harasses you or touches you inappropriately... and certain occasions when my inner caveman must claim you in primitive ways."

Her eyes sparked interest, but she refocused the conversation. "So you'll take the job?"

"My résumé is in your briefcase. Feel free to have the Board check all my references."

"I'm so glad we could lure you away from your job in Saint Louis," she whispered facetiously.

"The benefits here are infinitely better, I assure you, as is the view."

Kelsey shivered as his gaze raked over her body. She had loved running around naked before, but with her new breasts, she despaired of ever having to put clothes on again. With an inward grin, she wondered how a nude workplace environment would go over at Wings. Nah, probably not a good idea, particularly if Sebastian were working there—they'd never get anything done.

She stood and took her plate to the sink, then dropped her napkin into the trash.

When she returned to the dining room, Sebastian was gone. Panic shot through her, until she heard a big body flop onto her bed—*their* bed.

She found him spread eagle, diagonally across the mattress, his ever ready erection laying heavily across his belly.

Unconsciously she licked her lips as her pussy became wet, and she rounded the bed, ready to take delicious advantage of him.

But something on the floor beside his earlier-discarded clothes caught her eye. It was one of the smaller photos of the two of them in front of those gaudy green urns. She picked it up as she climbed onto the bed, then turned it over. On the back, Sebastian had neatly written her name and address, along with a quickly-scrawled note: *Find Kelsey ASAP. You love her with your life.*

"What's this?"

He sat up and looked at her, his expression tender. "Insurance. Just in case."

"Just in case what?"

"Kelsey, I *had* to come back to you. With or without the help of magic or memory."

"Without…memory?" She could barely get the word out around the sudden lump in her throat. "You would have given up everything?"

He touched her face, tears brimming in his eyes. "Everything is nothing without you."

Kelsey would have sworn she had no tears left after last night, but they slid down her cheeks nonetheless as she kissed him.

Sebastian returned her kiss, thanking the forces and the beings who orchestrated his assignment to Kelsey and allowed him to have her forever.

Then he made love to her with slow deliberation, pouring his soul into her with each brush of his lips, drinking her soul with each stroke of his tongue, knowing he had all the time in the world to treasure her, pleasure her.

"I want to stay like this forever," she whispered against his neck a long while later as she sat in his lap, straddling him, her hair trailing down his back, their juices seeping from where he still penetrated her.

Sebastian nodded and flexed himself inside her.

There were so many things he needed to tell her, so many things he had learned before returning to her that he needed to share. And a single question he needed to ask.

But he settled into the bed with her, pulling her into his embrace, nuzzling her neck as his heart bloomed with love for her. There would be plenty of time for sharing his knowledge later. They had several years at least before it would truly become imperative that she know what he now knew.

"We've got a long, long time to discover all that life together has to offer."

Epilogue

"Another disaster. Dammit Kelsey, it's been nearly four months! I swear you've jinxed me!"

Kelsey smiled sympathetically into the phone. "Gina, a date can be fun even if you don't intend to have sex."

"Yeah, okay, and I guess I had fun. I'm just getting tired of this dating crap is all. Seeing you so happy makes me want that, too. I wish I could find the perfect man and live happily ever after."

"Oh, I wish you could, too, hon. But do me a favor?"

"What?"

"Quit whining."

"What, I can't even feel sorry for myself now?"

"Maybe things will start looking up, you never know. Maybe the perfect man will magically poof into your life and you'll live blissfully ever after."

"Thanks so much for the sarcasm. Way to kick a girl when she's down."

"That wasn't sarcasm and you are anything but down. What did you tell me? We all hit dry spells? If you grin and bear it, you'll be smiling when the right man shows up."

"Okay, you're right. Four months is nothing compared to four *years*. I'll wait another couple months before I start whining again."

Kelsey laughed. "See? It's all in how you look at it." She looked at Sebastian, who had finished folding laundry—by *hand* even—and was now looking meaning-fully at her. "I've gotta go, Gina. I'll keep my fingers crossed for you."

"Okay. Bye sweetie."

"Bye hon." She replaced the phone in its cradle and sashayed into the living room, making her unbound breasts bounce slightly under her t-shirt.

"Sebastian?" she asked sweetly as she drew a finger over his chest.

"Hmm...?"

"Can I make a wish for someone else?"

"When have you ever done differently?"

"I don't mean food or clothing. I mean..."

"This wouldn't have anything to do with Gina's love life, would it?"

She pushed him to a sitting position in the easy chair and straddled him. "I really want her to be happy. She's miserable now that she knows what she's missing."

"And what exactly is she missing?"

"A man who fits her perfectly. Someone who's in-tense and edgy, even a little dangerous. Gentlemen abso-lutely bore her—she wants a man who takes what he wants and accepts no excuses. And he has to be big and hard all over, but intelligent, too."

He chuckled. "Edgy and dangerous? Rude and de-manding? I know somebody like that."

"Really?"

"Really."

"Oh, Sebastian, I wish Gina could find the same sort of love we have."

"Hmmm... Perhaps it's about time to return the fa-vor. He's been around a lot longer than me, so I'd say he's due for retirement."

"Is it Gabe?" She grinned. From what Sebastian had told her about him, she knew on some strange instinctual level that Gabe was everything her friend needed in a man.

Sebastian nodded. "Let me see what I can do. After all, a wish is a wish."

~The End~

Don't miss Gina's story!
Desperately Seeking Cupid
Coming soon!

For information on contributing to a backpack program in your area, please visit:

http://www.secondharvest.org/site_content.asp?s=57

 **DEVI SPARKS** has a dirty mind and loves to share it with her readers. A 'good girl' for most of her life and always a late bloomer, Devi didn't arrive at her rebellious teenage years until her late twenties.

Never one to waste a perfectly good rebellion, she is still savoring every unruly whim and notion (though not necessarily acting on them—wisdom and experience and all that 'grown up' stuff *sigh*) and hasn't looked back.

She's an EPPIE Finalist author (under another name in another genre), and is published in both fiction and non-fiction.

Devi currently lives in Texas and enjoys writing, painting, traveling, and well… other things ;-)

Readers may visit her online at www.DeviSparks.com

Come discover what else

 PHAZE

has to offer!

www.Phaze.com

Printed in the United States
47337LVS00001B/7-117